Shareem Series
By Allyson James

Rees

"I am truly moved by the obvious love these two characters feel for each other and anxiously await a sequel in this extremely satisfying world. Ms. James has created a masterpiece." — Just Erotic Romance Reviews, Gold Star Award

Calder

"*Calder* is a perfect Shareem novel, full of hot, exciting sex and perfect emotions from both characters. I fell in love with the dark, brooding Calder, who fought against feelings he long thought dead inside him." — *Joyfully Reviewed*

Braden

"I . . . enjoyed the clever weaving of the many layers in this tale into something I was pleased to find was deeper and more profound than it first seemed." — *Long and Short of It Reviews*

JUSTIN

TALES OF THE SHAREEM

ALLYSON JAMES

Chapter One

"Ident card."

The patroller who held her hand out to Justin had pretty brown eyes, sleek dark hair, and a lush body in a tight coverall he wouldn't mind seeing her out of. Not bad, but she was a patroller and right now in Justin's way.

He moved past her outstretched hand, making for the Vistara station's exit. "Sorry, sweetheart. Catch me on the way back."

The patroller got in front of him again. "I *said*, 'Ident card.'"

Even through his impatience, Justin noticed her smooth face, slightly upturned nose, and wide, kissable mouth. He was Shareem—of course he noticed. Her hair was pulled into an *I'm-a-tight-ass* knot on the back of her head, but she couldn't hide the sheen of it.

He didn't need to give her his ident card to leave the station. Justin had bought a ticket and already turned it in, like everyone else. But patrollers enjoyed hanging around hovertrain platforms harassing people, especially Shareem.

"Tell you what," Justin said. "You wait for me here, and I'll give you my ident card on my way back."

Dark brows snapped together, and her sultry eyes narrowed. "No, you'll give me your ident card *now*, and I'll think about letting you walk out of here."

Damn it. He was already late, and if he didn't hurry, Sybellie would be gone, and Justin would have to wait another entire day to see her. If Justin didn't see her every day, some space in his heart went empty.

He tried to stride around the patroller, but she got in front of him again. The little sweetie was fast. "Ident card," she repeated, a dangerous edge to her voice.

Fuck this.

Justin grabbed the woman around the waist, lifted her, swung around with her, and set her back on her feet. She gaped in shock as he plunked her down, too stunned to restrain him or even shout for help.

Justin grinned, tapped the end of her nose, whirled away, and strode through the crowd and out of the station—fast.

He heard her shouting behind him, but he didn't worry. The small female patroller would never out-stride a long-legged Shareem.

A loud *thrum* vibrated through his body, and something hot bit into his backside. Justin's knees buckled, and he met the pavement, face-first, his nerves sizzling like fried wires.

He heard applause. The crowd on the Vistara was cheering the patroller who'd taken down the dangerous Shareem.

Through his fogged vision Justin saw the patroller's booted feet stop in front of his face. Justin couldn't keep his gaze from traveling from her slim ankles up her long, sexy legs all the way to sweetly curved hips hugged by the coverall.

His last thought before another stun burst whacked him in the side was that she had the most lickable calves he'd ever seen in his life.

* * * * *

His name was Justin.

The information on Deanna's prisoner flickered across her console at the main Pas City detention facility.

He'd been part of DNAmo's Shareem project — genetically engineered males created for sexual pleasure — before DNAmo's productions had been declared illegal and the company forced to shut down. This Shareem — Justin — had been sold to a buyer a few years before the shutdown and shipped to a planet called Sirius III.

Sirius III had required the woman who'd purchased Justin to let him go, as human trafficking was highly illegal in the Sirius system. Justin, once free, had apparently decided to remain on Sirius. He'd lived there for twenty-five years as an ordinary citizen, cohabitating for about fifteen years with a woman called Shela, until her death a couple of years ago.

A few months ago, Justin had returned, of his own volition, to Bor Narga.

Why?

The Shareem represented all things sensual and sexual, qualities abhorred by most Bor Nargans. On Bor Narga, the forbidden Shareem were second class, restricted, watched, forced to take inoculations to keep them sterile and disease free.

So why had this Shareem given up his freedom to come back to this rock?

Deanna studied the holopic that rotated slowly on her console. Justin had dark brown hair, hard, handsome features, and, of course, Shareem-blue eyes. That was the man in her cell, all right.

The holopic showed only his upper torso, but Deanna filled in the rest. He'd towered over her in the train station, the man nearly seven feet tall. He'd worn sun-blocking robes over his tunic and leggings, but the material had outlined a body of solid muscle.

And he was strong. When the Shareem had lifted her, the power in his hands had taken her breath away, rendering her so hot and confused that she'd not even thought to draw her gun. Clipping handcuffs over his thick wrists had given her a strange shiver of pleasure as well.

Deanna hadn't been in the processing room when her male underlings had stripped him down. She was supposed to abhor the sexual as much as the next Bor Nargan woman, but *damn*. She'd liked to have seen that.

Deanna's console beeped, startling her out of her daydreams, the alert from the guard she'd been waiting for.

The Shareem was awake.

She shut down her files, tucked her handheld into her belt, and left for the detention area.

Pas City's detention building contained a maze of cells made of foot-thick transparent plasti-glass, each cell about six feet square and ten high. Nutrition gels were issued through a slot in the floor every few hours, refuse taken away through another slot. That was it.

The Shareem called Justin was in a cell halfway down an empty row. The guards had let him resume a loincloth that covered his privates, but nothing more. Apart from that, he wore only a black chain around his right biceps, the mark of the Shareem.

Those biceps were huge, his arms connected to equally large shoulders, round and tight, above a chest as sculpted with muscle. He was male beauty, slick with sweat, on display for all to see.

Deanna made herself approach his cell at a brisk walk, pretending that all that naked flesh didn't unnerve her. Justin raised his head as though he heard her coming, though the cells had been soundproofed.

He looked exhausted, dark smudges under his eyes, but then, he'd gotten a double dose from Deanna's stun weapon. In spite of appearing as though he could barely stand, however, he gave her an enraged look that could blow a hole through the foot-thick wall.

He said something, lips moving in silence behind the soundproofed wall. When Deanna flicked a switch to turn on the mikes between them, Justin closed his mouth, but he never took his eyes off her.

"You know that refusing an identification request from a patroller is grounds for incarceration, don't you?" Deanna asked. "Even termination?"

Justin folded his arms, all those muscles rippling. "Yeah? Well, fuck you, sweetheart."

Deanna made herself not flinch. "If you give me a good reason for refusing my request for identification, I might be able to get you a lighter sentence."

"Request?" His smile held no humor. "Is that what that was? You didn't need my ident card, Patroller. I'm in your damned database."

"I know that. But all Shareem must render identification when asked."

"You know, you're sexy with that rule book up shoved up your ass."

Deanna curled her fingers into her palms. "You had your ident card with you. Why didn't you just give it to me?"

He shrugged. "I was in a hurry."

"For what?"

Justin stepped forward, put his mouth right in front of the mike, and spoke slowly. "None of your damned business."

Deanna's gaze riveted to his mouth. His lips were pale and smooth, and the way he smiled made his tanned face delectable. His tongue moved with his words, red and moist . . .

She dragged in a breath. "You're Shareem. I'm a patroller. It *is* my business."

"Not this time."

His eyes were so blue. All Shareem had blue eyes, while native-born Bor Nargans had brown. Their irises were a little bigger than the average human's, and widened when they were aroused.

"Your record shows that you were warned twice to stay out of the Vistara district," Deanna said. "So why didn't you?"

"There's nothing in your rules that says I can't walk down a public street, sweetheart. I looked it up."

"But people on the Vistara have made it clear they don't want Shareem on their part of the hill."

"People on the Vistara are a bunch of full-of-themselves, sticks-up-their-asses, wannabe rich folks. You patrol there. You should know that."

Deanna privately agreed with him—patrolling the Vistara could be a major pain in the butt. Not because of crime, but because of the incessant complaints of the people who lived there. Nothing the patrollers did was ever good enough for them.

"Doesn't matter," she said. "You received several warnings to stay away. You knew you could get arrested if you went up there again. So why did you?"

"I don't know. Maybe I felt like moving the sticks in their asses."

Deanna forced herself not to smile. "Who did you go to see?"

Justin hesitated the slightest bit, and Deanna knew she'd hit pay dirt. She'd only guessed, but his little start confirmed it.

"None of your damned business," he said again.

"A woman who hired you?"

"Sure." He gave her a steady blue stare. "A client."

Shareem couldn't lie, the files said. They'd been programmed to have no emotions and no ability to lie—to have no understanding of the need to lie.

So why was she doubting him?

"Can this woman vouch for you?" Deanna asked.

Justin grinned, and again his face deepened into something beyond handsomeness. "A woman from the Vistara? Admitting she hired a Shareem? Are you kidding me?"

True—if a Vistara woman confessed to wanting sex, especially with a forbidden Shareem, her sticks-up-their-asses neighbors could make her a social outcast.

"You might die if she doesn't admit it," Deanna said.

"Guess it's not my lucky day, then."

What was wrong with him? Did he *want* to be terminated?

"Look, I can be discreet," she said. "I'll contact this woman privately. No one has to know I spoke to her or that she hired you. She can trust me not to reveal her name."

Justin leaned his forearms on the wall. "You're saying that if this client vouches for me, you'll let me go?"

"I can at least stop the termination order."

Justin remained where he was a moment longer, then he straightened up. "Nope. Sorry, darlin'. A Shareem doesn't kiss and tell."

Deanna made a noise of exasperation. "Gods, *why* are you being so stupid?"

They were going to kill him. This beautiful specimen of a man would be injected with drugs until he lost consciousness and died, then his prefect body would be incinerated.

Deanna reached to the transparent wall and spread her fingers across the cool plasti-glass. The gesture went against all her training, but for some reason she wanted to do it. She had to get through to him.

"I'm not supposed to tell you this," she said, "but the people on the Vistara wanted you to be terminated as soon as I slapped the cuffs on you. They didn't even want me to bring you down here and lock you up. I made the decision not to listen to them. You were my bust, *my* prisoner."

Justin's eyes flickered, and she saw a flash of serious anger in them. But Shareem couldn't get angry--could they? Not like this, not with murder in their eyes.

"Well, aren't you a love?" he said, his voice going soft. "Deciding that the poor Shareem gets to live?"

"If you sign a statement promising you'll never set foot in the Vistara district again—and *obey* it—I might be able to let you go."

He didn't hesitate. "No."

Deanna balled her fists. "What is the matter with you? Make the promise that you won't go up there again, and I might be able to get you free. Help me help you."

Justin came out of his negligent stance and slammed into the wall in front of her, fists against the plasti-glass. Deanna started to back up in alarm, but she made herself stay in place.

He couldn't hurt her, couldn't get out, couldn't even do the Shareem trick of using pheromones to relax her. The cell walls, set up to contain any kind of prisoner, including off-worlders who might have telepathy, wouldn't let him.

"You're only offering to 'help' me so you can sign off on your fucking report," he said in a hard voice. *"The Shareem wouldn't cooperate, so he had to die.* Not your fault—you followed the rules. That's all you want, Patroller."

"Deanna."

"What?"

"My name isn't *Patroller*. It's Deanna. Deanna Surrell, Patroller First Class."

He stared down at her. "You trying to be my friend now . . . *Deanna*?"

He pronounced the name carefully, his voice taking on a sensuality that reached through the glass.

"I'm not trying to be your friend," Deanna said, softening her tone. "But I don't want to see you terminated because some sticks-up-their-asses, wannabe rich folks decided you ruined their pristine street. That's not fair. But I can't help you if you won't work with me." Deanna put her hand on the transparent wall again, directly over one of his fists. "Please, Justin."

Chapter Two

The *please* got to him.

This had to be a first. A patroller saying *please* to a Shareem.

Her brown eyes had warmed, and the hand placed directly over his was a sweet gesture. She'd look beautiful with a scarf around her wrists, she on her knees, begging him with that look in her eyes.

Deanna. Lovely name. Justin could whisper it while he cupped her breasts, again while he slid his hand down to find the wet heat of her pussy.

His cock tightened, and Justin immediately shut off his thoughts. The last thing he needed was a big hard-on, here in these cells where he couldn't hide it.

"Sign the statement, and you can go," Deanna said. "As easy as that."

Justin rested his forehead against the transparent wall. He'd not negated her assumption that he'd been on his way to visit a client, because he sure as hell wasn't about to tell this patroller the real reason he'd gone to the Vistara.

And no way would Justin sign a document promising he'd stay away from the district. Not while Sybellie lived there.

Sybellie, his daughter.

Shareem were not allowed, on pain of death, to father children. If Justin had to be terminated to protect the knowledge that Sybellie was the offspring of a Shareem, so be it.

Sybellie did not know that Justin was her biological father and neither did her adoptive parents. He would never let that knowledge out, because the gods only knew what the asshole women in the Bor Nargan government would do to Sybellie if they found out she carried Shareem DNA.

They might shut her away, experiment on her, dissect her, or simply kill her. Justin wouldn't risk that, not even to save his own life.

But, damn it, she was his *daughter*. He wanted to see her. He needed to see her, even for a brief hour across a crowded street.

"Please, Justin," Deanna said.

That *please* again. It did funny things to his insides, even through his worry and anger.

Maybe if Justin did please this patroller, she'd let him out and dismiss the case. He could please her with a little screwing, maybe in her cubicle, on her desk. He didn't have his box of equipment with him, but he could make do with a piece of cloth for her mouth, maybe a belt for hand restraints. Level-two Shareem were good at improvising.

Deanna's handheld beeped.

"Excuse me," she said.

A patroller being polite to a Shareem. What a day.

Deanna touched a button on the handheld and read whatever text was flowing to her, her mouth pursed.

A sweet, red mouth, with moist, plump lips. Nice for kissing and other things that mouths were good for.

Justin couldn't stop himself thinking these things, even with her holding his fate in her hands. He'd love it if she could hold something else in her hands too. It would make his inevitable termination all the sweeter.

Deanna snapped off the handheld. When she looked at him, the sympathy in her eyes had been replaced by a hard, angry glare. "You have friends in high places."

Justin had no idea what she was talking about. "Yeah?"

"I've been ordered to let you go, all charges dropped." And didn't she look pissed off about that?

"I guess it's not *your* lucky day, darlin'."

Deanna's voice went crisp. "The order comes from none other than the ruling family. Is one of them another client of yours?"

Justin said nothing. If the order came from the ruling family, he had a pretty good idea who'd told them to do it. He knew only one member of that family, a pretty lady called Brianne, who'd hooked up with not one, but two Shareem. Looks like it helped to have Shareem friends who were regularly fucking powerful women.

"Yes, yes, I know." Deanna sounded disgusted. "You don't kiss and tell." She pushed buttons on her handheld. "If this holds up my promotion, Shareem, I swear to the gods I will make your life hell. I might make your life hell just for the fun of it."

No more, *Please, Justin,* no more first names.

Too bad. The sincerity in her eyes had been there. The anger she showed now was outrage that someone had stomped on her authority and made her look stupid. Justin could almost feel sorry for her.

Almost.

Justin pressed a wet kiss to the glass and laughed when she whirled around and strode away.

"I'm looking forward to it, sweetheart," he called after her.

* * * * *

"Brianne," Justin said many hours later as he lifted yet another glass of ale. He was drunk, unsteady, and didn't care. "Let me kiss you. Can I kiss you?"

Brianne d'Aroth, granddaughter of the woman who ruled Bor Narga and advocate for Shareem rights, glared up at him. "No. Justin, you idiot."

"Sounds like my baby's pissed at you." Aiden, Brianne's asshole level-one Shareem lover, stopped and grinned at Justin. Blond Aiden had been face sculpted, and his features were a work of art.

Aiden slid his arm around Brianne and kissed her cheek. "You do *not* want to get this lady mad at you, Justin, trust me."

"Why not?" Justin slurred. "She won't go down on you when she's mad?"

"Nope, she can be a real bitch about it. Won't even watch Ky do it to me either."

"Aiden, my friend, your life is pure hell," Justin said.

Justin was a little more sanguine than the other Shareem about the relationship between Aiden and Ky—two Shareem who'd gone from being best friends to being lovers. On Sirius, all kinds of relationships were accepted, fully legal, and not considered shocking, as long as everyone involved was adult and consenting.

Brianne heaved a sigh. "Will you two be serious? I had to pull every string I had to get you out of prison, Justin. If I hadn't, you'd be marching to the termination chamber even now. I had to give my word that you'd never go up to the Vistara again. Do you understand me?"

"I understand." Justin took a last slurp of ale and stared morosely at the bottom of the glass. "Days like these I miss Sirius, boring as it was."

"So why did you come back here?" Aiden asked. "You never have come up with a good explanation."

"Because it's none of your damned business." Justin had to keep saying that. Maybe someday someone would listen to him.

"That's true," Aiden said. "But you've got us curious."

Red-haired Judith, who owned the bar, snatched Justin's ale glass from the table but didn't give him another one. "Leave Justin alone. He's had an ordeal."

Justin slid his arm around Judith's waist as she cleared the table. "*This* is why I came back to Bor Narga. Because I heard about this great bar owned by a sexy lady named Judith."

"Bullshit," Judith said, but she smiled.

Justin slid his hand downward until he could give her ass a little fondle. Judith pulled away, but not in anger.

"Don't," she said. "Mitch doesn't like it."

Aiden, Justin, and another Shareem called Braden, who'd strolled up, said "Oooo," at the same time. Aiden added, "Mitch doesn't like it."

Judith blushed while they laughed. Mitch was a human, off-world pilot who'd taken to coming to Judith's bar. He'd also taken to Judith. Justin hadn't heard that Mitch had asked Judith to be exclusive, but good for her.

Braden, the black-haired Shareem who'd just arrived, slid himself onto a stool at Justin's table. Justin had shared an apartment with Braden when he'd first returned to Bor Narga, but had moved out when Braden's new lover, Elisa, moved in.

"I'm glad for Judith," Braden said as Judith walked away. "She deserves someone special after having Shareem manhandle her for years."

"Not that I ever heard her complain," Aiden said.

Justin said, "But does Mitch keep *his* hands off other ladies when he's not here? He needs to play fair."

"I say we ask him," Aiden said.

"Good idea," Braden said. "We need to make sure he's good enough for our Judith."

"*Excuse me,*" Brianne said loudly. "I notice how deftly you all managed to change the subject. I need to know *why* I had to pull rank to get Justin out of jail this afternoon."

"Let it rest, Bree," Braden said. "It was a patroller getting her panties in a twist and taking it out on Justin. Besides, Justin's not used to taking orders. He actually got to live like a human being for a while. He probably pissed off the patroller by not kissing her ass when she told him to."

Justin nodded, as though Braden had nailed it.

Braden and Elisa were the only people on the planet, besides Rees, who knew the true reason that Justin had returned. They'd all kept it quiet, even from the other Shareem, understanding that the less their friends knew, the safer it would be for all concerned.

Brianne made another noise of annoyance but gave up, and Justin let out his breath in silent relief.

Aiden pulled Brianne against him and kissed her hair. "You know, baby, I'm in the mood for some rough play. How about we go find Ky and let him have his way with us? Then when he's done, I'll soothe it all better."

Brianne blushed, but she looked ready for what he wanted. Aiden was a level one, pure sensuality—scented oils, massages, slow sex. Ky, on the other hand, was a level three, which meant bondage play—varying from easy to hardcore, depending on what the lady wanted. Aiden and Ky balanced each other perfectly, opposite and complementary at the same time.

Aiden led Brianne out of the bar, and Braden and Justin watched them go.

"Sometimes I wonder what the three of them do together," Braden said. "And sometimes I just don't want to know."

"Hey, it works for them," Justin said.

"And I'm good with that." Braden took drink, wiped his mouth, and leaned in to Justin. "But seriously, why did you go up to the Vistara again?"

Justin's head started to ache. "I wanted to see her."

"If you get yourself executed, my friend, you won't see her at all."

"I know." Justin tilted his chair back on two legs and leaned against the wall. "I want so bad to see her, and at the same time, it kills me to."

Braden gave him a sympathetic look. "You found Lillian, yet?"

Sybellie's mother. Justin had returned to Bor Narga to find them both. "No. Nothing."

"Elisa hasn't turned anything up either," Braden said. "But don't worry. Elisa's the best librarian on the planet. If there's a record, she'll find it."

"It's getting bloody impossible."

"Don't give up yet, my friend. We'll find her."

Braden could afford to be optimistic. He'd paired off with Elisa not long after Justin's return. Justin was glad for him, but their happiness gave him a lonely feeling. Justin had lived with a woman on Sirius—Shela—for fifteen years, and they'd been lovers and best friends. He missed her like crazy.

Justin needed to change the subject. "What's it like for your lady, living with you and your jokes all the time? Who ever heard of a cheerful Dom?"

Braden grinned. "Hey, she loves me. Anyway, isn't that what level twos do? Spank and laugh?"

"Fun and games. Whipped cream and furry handcuffs."

Braden shook his head. "Boring. Fake bondage."

"Bondage-Light," Justin corrected. He pushed himself from his chair. "I'm outta here. Judith has cut me off, and I need some sleep."

"Take it easy out there," Braden said, expression serious. "Brianne can't always be around to cover your ass."

"Don't worry. I learned my lesson."

Like hell he had.

Braden watched with a skeptical look as Justin said good night to Judith and got himself out of the bar. Justin had taken the apartment next door to the bar—with Judith's help—a tiny place, but there he could shut out the world and get some peace.

Justin went inside, stripped off, showered, dried himself, and landed facedown on his bed. The excess of ale sent him quickly to sleep.

He dreamed of a patroller with pretty eyes and sexy ankles threatening him with a gun loaded with whipped cream. He was naked, and so was she.

The whipped cream dripped coolly across his back and down his body. He felt a hot tongue licking and licking, teeth on his ass, as she ate the whipped cream from him, dollop by dollop.

Then the patroller with the big brown eyes turned him over and smiled at him, right before she wrapped that beautiful mouth around his cock.

She suckled and stroked, tongue tickling the underside and driving him crazy. Justin got harder and harder, his hips rocking as she suckled him. Gods, it felt good. *Harder, baby, harder.*

Justin wanted to taste her in return. He'd spread her legs, dribble the whipped cream across her pussy, bury his face in her, and lick her clean.

In his dream, he heard the click of handcuffs, felt the familiar velvet of his lined ones around his own wrists. She put the loaded whipped cream gun against his temple.

"No, Shareem. I do this *my* way."

Her way meant squirting whipped cream all over his chest, then licking down to his cock. Swirling her tongue around the tip, the heat of her mouth closing around him. Squeeze, suck. *Yes.*

Come. I want to come. Justin wanted to mark her with his seed, so she'd know she belonged to him.

And then she'd arrest him. She already had him in cuffs. Maybe she'd swat his ass, making it sting, before she cooled it down with whipped cream. Then she'd lick him again. He'd like that.

Justin would break free, and he'd catch her when she tried to get away, and do it all back to her . . .

A heavy buzzing cut through his dream. What the fuck? Maybe the whipped cream gun was overloading.

Another buzzing, sharper, more insistent. It shattered the dream like glass, and the pleasant sensations vanished into smoke.

Justin opened his eyes. He found his hand around his throbbing cock, his head pounding just as hard. He peeled his aching hand from his penis and reached for his hangover pills.

Another buzzing. The front door. *Shit.*

Justin rolled out of bed, pulled a tunic over his nakedness, and stumbled into the front room. He slammed the door open. "What?"

He'd expected Braden, or maybe Rees. What he got was his sexy patroller, Deanna, who walked right in past him.

"I need to talk to you," she said.

Chapter Three

"Come in." Justin said to the open door. "Make yourself at home."

Deanna looked around the small living room strewn with Justin's clothes and other junk. Shela had always yelled at Justin to clean up, but without her to motivate him, Justin had lost interest.

"You *live* here?" Deanna asked.

Justin let the door slam. "No, I stand in the middle of this room for the hell of it."

Deanna peered into the corner kitchen then at the alcove that led to his bedroom and bathroom.

"It's very small."

"It's claustrophobic. But I didn't have a choice." Few wanted to rent to Shareem. He'd been lucky to get this.

"My superiors came down hard on me about you," Deanna said. "Getting a call from on high to let you go embarrassed them. So, they're taking it out on me. Unless I can prove I had good cause to arrest you, my promotion is off, and I might even be demoted. I make another mistake, and I'm out."

Stupid Bor Nargans. They trained their patrollers to be major pains in the ass, and then got mad at them for doing their jobs.

"Not your fault, sweetheart," he said. "Shareem are shitheads. Everyone knows that."

She shot him a wry smile. "I don't think that will be good enough for my superior."

Her voice, even agitated, was sexy. Maybe she really did have whipped cream in her stun gun.

"What do you want me to tell you? That I went there to climb through a woman's bedroom window to ravish her senseless? So you can arrest me for real and make it stick?"

"I'm not going to arrest you at all. I only need to prove that you were let off because of favoritism, not incompetence on the part of the patrollers. Particularly incompetence on the part of Patroller First Class Deanna Surrell."

Justin never thought he'd feel sorry for a patroller, but with his mind full of the dream, Deanna's dismay aroused Justin's sympathy.

In the three months Justin had been back on Bor Narga, the patrollers had followed him, carded him, harassed him, watched him. They'd done the same to his friends. They were a body of condescending, sneering bitches in coveralls.

Deanna's uniform was tight on her body, and again she wore her dark hair in the severe bun all patrollers did. But with her eyes holding anger and worry, she looked almost human.

Justin gathered up clothes from the couch, dumped them in a corner, and gestured to the battered sofa. "Sit down."

She sat but scooched to the end of the couch when Justin sat right next to her.

He laughed. "Are you afraid of me?"

"No." Her eyes betrayed the lie. "I have my stun gun."

Justin went hot. "Did you load it with whipped cream?"

"What?"

"I had a dream about you last night. You and furry handcuffs."

Now panic warred with her interest. "You put me in handcuffs?"

"No." Justin stretched his arm across the back of the couch, letting his fingers dangle an inch from her shoulder. "*I* was in the handcuffs. I guess deep down I wanted to play some games with you."

"What does that mean, exactly?"

"In my dream, you locked my hands around my bedpost, and you bit my bare ass. Then you squirted whipped cream all over my cock and sucked it off."

Deanna's eyes went wide, and he sensed her body warming. "I could arrest you for even saying that to me."

"Little tease. Did you bring real handcuffs? Maybe I could turn the tables and put the cuffs on you."

"I'm warning you, Justin. I can throw your butt in jail just for talking to me like this."

Justin leaned closer, his blood heating in a way it hadn't in a long, long time. "Then my friends in high places will get me out again, and you'll be back here in my apartment trying to save your job. Full circle."

Her anger flashed. "That doesn't mean you can get away with anything you want."

"Sure as hell sounds like it to me, sweetheart." Justin moved his fingers closer to her, letting them rest a fraction of an inch from her coverall. "If it makes you feel better, it's programmed into Shareem that we can't touch a lady until they give us permission. We can cajole and talk and promise, but until you say yes, we can't do anything."

Deanna let out a breath, warm on his hand. "That's true."

"So you're safe from me, Patroller. Don't worry."

Justin didn't mention that he'd learned to break that programming during his years on Sirius. He'd had no intention of forcing a woman, but Shela, a workaholic, had kept ignoring Justin's blatant hints that she should start a sexual relationship with him.

Shela had been so good at playing hard to get that Justin had trained himself to make the first move. He'd spent nights of sweat and pain before he'd convinced his body to let him do it. And he'd done it, to Shela's surprise and delight.

"So as soon as you want me to get the furry handcuffs, you tell me," he said.

"No." The answer was clipped.

"Damn, I hate when a woman is all business."

"Live with it. And tell me why you went to the Vistara."

Justin propped his elbow on the back of the sofa, head on his fist. Keeping your hands near your face distracted people, he'd learned. They didn't watch your eyes.

"See, Patroller, the reason ladies like Shareem is . . . we're discreet."

Deanna's gaze sharpened, and Justin could almost feel the click of the cuffs. "You'd go to jail to protect this woman's identity?"

"Why not? I already have once."

"She must be some woman."

"Must be, yeah."

Was that envy in her eyes? He hoped so. His patroller wasn't bad. Now if he could get her to take down that bun of steel and relax.

"So you did go up there to visit a woman," Deanna said.

"I never said that."

"She invited you?"

"Never said that either."

Deanna folded her arms, which pushed up the cleavage that would show if she undid the coverall. "What you're telling me, Justin, is that you violated two warnings to stay out of the district in order to meet an unknown woman at an undisclosed place. You should have explained to her that you weren't allowed to go up there."

Justin rubbed the wall next to his head. "See, the tricky thing is, if I tell you I went to ravish a Vistara woman, so yeah, you were right to arrest me — then I'll be back in my boring cell. It's not in my best interest to help you."

"But I *order* you to help me."

She sounded so desperate that Justin laughed.

"Tell you what. I'll level with you." *I'll sort of lie to you.* "I went back up to the Vistara because the last two times I was there, I saw this patroller in the train station. She had pretty brown eyes and hair the color of midnight. I wish she'd let her hair down. I bet it would be beautiful."

Deanna's eyes softened for a fraction of a second. "Don't bullshit me, Shareem."

"No bullshit. I bet your hair really does look good."

"That's not what I meant."

He let his smile go sensual. "Take your hair down. I dare you."

"No."

Justin leaned forward a little, looking straight into her eyes. "You take it down, and I'll tell you who I went to see. Promise."

* * * * *

Deanna chewed her lip, very aware of Justin's large, warm body inches from hers. No foot-thick plasti-glass to protect her now.

He was different from what she'd thought he would be—he was smart, with a sense of humor that was almost playful. But the blue filling his eyes as he watched her reminded Deanna that he'd been created in a factory, not born, not quite human.

Would it be worth it to do what he said? He wasn't asking for anything sexual, only for her to release her hair. Deanna did that every day when she got home from work anyway. It might be worth it to get a straight answer from him.

She reached up and touched the clasp that held her bun in place. Justin leaned toward her, as though Deanna taking down her hair was the most important thing in the world to him.

Deanna slowly released the clasp and let her hair, fine and straight, tumble past her shoulders.

"Beautiful," Justin said, voice low, gaze only for her. "Like the swaths of silk I see in the markets. Black silk."

Deanna's breath hitched. "It's only hair."

Justin stretched his arm across the back of the sofa, again stopping shy of touching her. She swore she could feel sparks between his fingers and her skin.

"It's beauty," Justin said. "Why do you hide it?"

"I can't do my job with my hair in my face, can I?" Deanna meant to sound stern, but her voice cracked.

"You wouldn't need your stun gun. All you'd have to do was smile, and the perps would drop at your feet."

What was he talking about? All *he* had to do was smile, and he'd have women on their knees.

Justin was smiling now, the little twitch of lips that warmed his eyes and made Deanna's temperature jump to scalding level. This was dangerous.

Justin reached out and wound his finger through a strand of her hair.

"Stop that," she said.

Justin took his time about obeying. He smoothed the lock with his fingers, tugged it gently, and finally released it.

"It feels as beautiful as it looks," he said.

Deanna shivered, a deep, soul-licking shiver. "All right, I did what you asked. Now, tell me who you went to the Vistara to see."

"Okay, I lied about that part. I'm not going to tell you."

"What?" Deanna shoved him aside and jumped to her feet. "But I did what you asked."

He opened his hands. "I'm Shareem, sweetie. I seduce. It's what I do. And I wanted to see what you looked like with your hair down."

"Why?"

"Because I knew you'd be damned sexy."

Deanna's throat tightened. She could almost believe him when he said it like that. *Sexy.* No one had ever called her that. No one would ever dare.

But Shareem were masters of seduction, and seduction involved lies. Shareem weren't supposed to be able to lie . . . but Justin had done it. He'd promised to tell her what she wanted to know and then reneged. Look at him, lounging on the sofa like a decadent god, daring her to take him down for being what he was.

Deanna started to wind her hair back into its bun, but she dropped the clasp, which clinked on the bare floor. She dove for it at the same time Justin came off the couch and reached for it.

Their shoulders collided, his a solid wall of muscle. He steadied her with hands that were incredibly gentle. "You all right?" he asked.

"Yes." She gasped. "Don't touch me."

If he didn't let go, she'd never get to her feet, never regain her balance.

Justin held on to her even more firmly as he helped her to stand. "You need to be touched, Deanna," he said. "You're crying out for it."

Deanna stared at him a frozen moment, her body agreeing with him. Warmth tickled between her thighs, and she wanted him to hold on to her and never let go.

But he only released her and handed her the clip. The sudden absence of his warmth was like being doused in cold water.

Deanna wound up her hair and snapped the clasp. "I'll be watching you, Shareem. I'll find out what you're up to. You won't be able to walk outside without tripping over me."

His smile flashed. "Promise?"

The smile made something raw boil up inside her. She had to get out of there.

Justin made it to the door before she did, slamming his hand to the doorframe. "Don't be afraid of me, Deanna." Again, his voice was gentle, coercing.

Deanna patted her stun gun with a shaking hand. "I'm not afraid. I'm armed."

"Seriously. I'd never hurt you." Justin's gaze locked to hers. "And thank you."

"For what? Coming here to question you?"

"For letting me see what you look like."

Deanna's answer died on her lips. His body was incredibly warm, his heat like a blanket, and he wasn't even touching her.

Deanna punched the control to open the door. They looked at each other for another long moment, something passing between them that Deanna didn't understand.

Then Deanna ducked under his arm and walked swiftly out of the apartment. The Bor Nargan sunshine blinded her, but weirdly it felt nowhere near as hot as Justin had.

Justin didn't say good-bye. Deanna turned around to discover why not, but the door slammed, and she stood alone in the street, facing blank, rusting metal.

* * * * *

Deanna dreamed about him that night.

In the dream, she entered a room to find Justin naked and tied to a chair. He sat casually, as he had on the sofa, but now his hands were fastened behind his back, his body stretched out for her to see. His cock was long and straight, fully erect, stretching upward from a cross of ropes.

"Deanna," he said in his dark voice. "Let your hair down for me."

Without hesitation, Deanna pulled the clasp from the bun. Her hair cascaded, thick and curly, all the way to her feet . . . *Well, this is a dream.*

"Thank you," Justin said. "You're beautiful. Now, come here."

She moved to him, her bare feet sinking into soft carpet. Deanna was wearing little, only a silk sheath over bare skin.

Justin watched her as she stopped in front of him, his smile spreading. His body was rock hard with muscle, slick with perspiration, and that cock . . . . It stood straight up, rising with every breath.

"Take off your dress," he said.

Without argument, Deanna unclasped the silk sheath and let it slide to the floor.

Justin skimmed his gaze up and down her, eyes hot blue. "Untie me, sweetheart."

"No." Deanna smiled. This was *her* dream, and she was in charge.

"Please." Perspiration wet his forehead. "I want to touch you."

"No," she whispered.

Her Shareem. Tied up for her. Wanting her.

Deanna went to him and daringly straddled his thighs, her legs on either side of his. His cock was so big, and dark with wanting, so close . . .

"Have a seat, baby," Justin said.

Should she? She could feel the warmth of him, even in her dream. His breath was hot on her skin. Delectable.

Deanna could do anything she wanted in this vision, and no one would ever know. It would be her secret passion, her fantasy.

"Down," he whispered.

This was insane. *He* was the one tied to the chair—Deanna should have all the power. His beautiful body was bound, his muscles tight as he strained against the ropes.

But Deanna felt compelled to obey him. She sat gingerly down on him, gasping when his cock slid up into her very wet opening.

Yes.

Deanna whimpered, but it was a sob of joy.

Justin lifted his hips, pushing all the way up inside her. Deanna knew it was a dream, but she still felt him, big and hard, reaching into her. Wonderful. She burned, but her sheath was wet and slick.

Justin watched her, his eyes so blue, the same way he'd watched her when they'd been on his couch. The simple act of him touching her hair had melted every part of her. Hence the dream.

This hot, fabulous, wicked dream.

The mad friction drove her on, the sinful look in Justin's eyes driving her as wild.

The image began to dissolve, Justin drifting away from her. Deanna was waking up. *No.*

She moaned his name as wildness poured over her in waves. She'd never felt anything like it before—darkness, and nothing but one point of *feeling*.

Deanna gasped and opened her eyes. She lay in the middle of her bed, alone, the sheets shoved aside. One of her hands pressed between her legs, her first two fingers solidly inside her.

She froze, habitual shame dashing over her. She'd touched herself, brought herself to orgasm. Taboo. Shameful.

Why? the rebellious part of her demanded. *It's heaven.*

She moved her fingers inside her sheath. The crazy wildness had faded, but the pressure inside her was still hot and satisfying.

Deanna stroked herself a little longer, calming down, comforting herself. But she knew that her own hands would be nowhere near as comforting as Justin's.

Gods, she wanted him. Deanna groaned again, cupping hard between her legs.

She'd have to live without him. Part of Deanna's job was to protect other women from Shareem, to make sure the walking sex machines didn't step out of line. She couldn't bring Justin to her bed and do her job.

She'd get over it. She'd make sure Justin stayed off the Vistara, and then she'd move on to other matters and forget about him.

Forget about him. Sure.

If she was so determined to forget, why did she imagine Justin's large, workworn hand pressing hard into her pussy as she drifted back into a troubled sleep?

* * * * *

"Anything?" Justin asked Elisa.

He stood with her in a small back room of a Pas City library, with Elisa peering at a terminal screen and Braden lounging against the desk. This library didn't have much in the way of resources, but if anyone could wrest information from the Bor Nargan databases, it was Elisa n'Arell.

"I'm sorry," Elisa said at last. "There's no record anywhere of the woman called Lillian. The last mention of her is of her quitting DNAmo and moving back home, where she obviously is not now. She lived in the apartment with her parents until their death, but she's gone now."

"Sybellie's birth was recorded," Justin said. "And her adoption. Lillian sent me a message about it."

He pulled out a plastic strip and held it up, the imprint of the precious message he'd saved. He thanked the gods he hadn't had it with him when cute little Patroller First Class Deanna Surrell had arrested him.

"The birth is recorded in a free clinic in the lower end of Pas City," Elisa said, reading her screen. "The mother didn't give a name."

Braden asked, "Isn't that illegal on Bor Narga?"

"Technically, yes," Elisa said. "But the attending medic might have not pressed the issue. Some lower-class women can't afford to raise a child, so they have them anonymously and give them up. That must have been very hard for Lillian to do."

"Yeah. It was."

And damn hard for Justin. He'd known that Lillian had been pregnant—she'd told him, and he'd advised her to quit DNAmo before they found out—but he'd been sent off before Lillian had given birth.

"May I see the message?" Elisa asked. "There might be something in it, if you don't mind."

Justin rubbed the plastic strip with his thumb. "It's encrypted. We'd figured out a way to send word to each other while she was at DNAmo. Lillian used that code."

"We can read it here if you input the key," Elisa said.

Justin hesitated. Elisa was right—she might be able to find something Justin hadn't seen, but it was difficult to hand over the slip. He'd told Elisa and Braden the story, but sharing the message was like sharing a very intimate part of himself.

Elisa gave him an understanding look as she took the slip and gently fed it into the slot. The computer screen filled with a string of numbers and letters, Lillian's code.

Justin leaned over Elisa, tapped in the key to break the code, and stood back as the message revealed itself.

We have a daughter, healthy and strong. She has been adopted by a family on the Vistara, one that will take good care of her. Be well, my friend. Our daughter is beautiful.

The screen blurred, and Justin touched the words with his fingertips.

Elisa studied the screen for a long time, then she keyed it off and removed the card. Her own eyes held tears as she gave it back to Justin.

"I'm so sorry," she said.

Justin tucked the plastic into his pocket, keeping it safe.

Braden cleared his throat. "I hate to say this, Jus, but maybe you should let it go. Maybe Lillian doesn't want to be found."

"I want to see her," Justin said stubbornly. "Even if it's only to tell her that Sybellie is all right, that she's beautiful."

"You need closure," Elisa said. "Finality."

"Yeah." Justin nodded as he pulled on his sunblocking robes. "That's it."

Braden chuckled. "My librarian, she loves the big words."

"Do you think you can find the medic who delivered Sybellie?" Justin asked, ignoring Braden. "Maybe she would have some idea where Lillian had been heading after that."

"I can try," Elisa said. "But the medic might have passed away or moved off planet by now."

"True. But it's all I've got."

Elisa patted his arm. "Don't worry, Justin. I won't give up. Katarina might be better at talking to the back-street medics. Do you mind if I ask her? I don't have to tell her specifically why."

"Sure." Justin took a breath. "If I have to bring her in on the secret, I will. Not Calder, though."

"Oh, right," Braden said. "Have a secret with Katarina on the sly, and see what happens to you."

"And you're not possessive about Elisa?" In spite of his sorrow, Justin wanted to grin at his friend. "Look at you hovering around while I'm here."

Braden gave a mock snarl and closed his big hands on Elisa's shoulders. "You keep your furry handcuffs to yourself."

"You're funny, Braden." Justin leaned down and kissed Elisa's cheek. "Thanks, Elisa. I owe you."

"No, you don't," she said. "It's my pleasure."

Justin gave Elisa's backside a pat, laughed at Braden's growl of possessiveness, swirled his robes around his shoulders, and left the library through the back door.

Once out in the sunny street, Justin walked to where Deanna lurked around the corner. He'd seen her follow him from his apartment, and now here she was, waiting for him to come out of the library.

Justin walked straight at her. Deanna tried to slip out of the alley before he got there, but Justin made it first and blocked her in with his body.

"Hey, sweetheart," he said. "Imagine running into you."

Chapter Four

Deanna made herself meet his gaze, standing straight and not flinching. "I didn't realize Shareem liked libraries so much," she said.

"We do when our best friend's girl is the librarian."

Justin wouldn't move. The alley behind her was a dead end, and if Deanna wanted walk out of it, she'd have to push past Justin. She knew that's exactly what he wanted, so she stayed put.

"And what were you in the library to look up?" Deanna asked.

He gave her a deadpan look. "Weather cycles in the Sand Sea. Maybe."

"Don't B.S. me. I can always get a warrant."

"I was there to visit my friends," he said. "That's all, sweetheart. Nothing illegal about that."

"You can visit them in that Shareem bar."

"Judith's? Sure, but my librarian friend can't always get away. She's nice. You'd like her."

Deanna tried a disdainful look but couldn't quite manage it. "She consorts with Shareem."

"*Consorts*." Justin laughed. "Is that what the kids are calling it these days? She lives with Braden, sure. I bet they have lots of sex. In fact, I know they do. I've seen them at it."

Deanna gaped at him. "*Seen* them? That's—" She wasn't sure how to feel about it. "—not right."

"A little voyeurism never hurt anyone, as long as everyone knows it's happening. You should try it sometime."

"*No.*"

"No?" Justin was somehow closer to her without her realizing he'd moved. "All right, then, what do you like to do?"

"Nothing. I mean, you shouldn't talk about things like that."

"I'm Shareem. I was bred to talk about things like that. Some people talk about politics—the gods know why. I talk about sex."

"Not to a patroller."

"Why not?" How did he get even closer? Justin's body heat enveloped her like a blanket, even under the scorching sun.

"If you want to follow me around," he said, "then you have to put up with what you get. Tell you what—instead of following me, walk with me, and I'll show you what I do all day."

All day. Walking with him strong and tall beside her, exuding that sexual charm.

Deanna had needs, she didn't deny it. Her dreams were enough to tell her that. But she also had work, responsibilities, and people to worry about.

But then, she needed to prove that this Shareem had broken the law, that Patroller First Class Deanna Surrell hadn't been wrong to arrest him. She needed to keep her job, or things could get very bad.

Justin was up to something, that was certain. Sticking with him would eventually lead her to what.

She looked Justin straight in his Shareem-blue eyes. "All right. Let's go. Where to next?"

Justin looked briefly surprised, as though he hadn't expected her to agree. Then his smile flashed again. "You have guts, Deanna. I'll give you that."

His tone was so admiring that Deanna found herself flushing with pleasure. She had no business flushing with pleasure, but she couldn't help it. His smile was so warm, his gaze all for her.

He held out his hand. "Come on then."

Deanna looked at his callused palm then back up at him in amazement. "I'm a patroller. I can't go walking around holding hands with a Shareem."

"Aw, poor thing." Justin wriggled his fingers then he lowered his hand to his side. "You'll just have to keep up then."

He turned abruptly and strode away, his long legs taking him swiftly into the Pas City crowd.

Deanna jogged after him. The man moved *fast*.

Justin ducked into a shaded alley full of vendors selling all kinds of cloth and inexpensive jewelry. Silk and gauze of all shades spilled from boxes and carts, semiprecious stones and silver glimmered from others. The woman in Deanna wanted to slow down and browse. The patroller in her needed to keep her quarry in sight.

Justin stopped in front of a vendor selling veils similar to those that highborn women wore—fabric that could merely frame the face or be pulled across eyes, nose, and mouth to keep out dust.

Justin was lifting a crimson veil from the table when Deanna panted up to him. "Wait," she said breathlessly.

"This would look nice on you," Justin said.

Before Deanna could protest, he draped the silk over her head and crossed the ends on her chest.

The silk brushed Deanna's face, the fabric touching her like a whisper. The vendor motioned to a mirror propped up on his table, and she couldn't resist taking a look.

Deanna, used to the drab gray of her patroller's uniform—which she wore with pride—was surprised at what she saw. The red of the veil brought color to her cheeks and made her eyes look darker. Her black hair, though drawn back tightly as usual, looked soft where it peeped out from under the veil. The silk complemented her hair rather than hid it, rendering it a brush of darkness beneath the cloth.

"This is lovely." The words came out before she could stop them.

"How much?" Justin asked the vendor.

"Twenty."

Deanne reluctantly slid off the veil and shook her head. "No, I can't afford . . ."

She faltered as Justin took a credit strip from his pocket and handed it to the vendor. The vendor zipped it through his handheld and made the transaction before Deanna could complete her sentence.

"Justin, you can't do that."

"I just did." Justin took his credit strip back, plucked the veil from Deanna's hands, and set it back over her head, laying the crossed ends over her shoulders.

"I can't accept this," Deanna said. "You can't *bribe* me."

The vendor glanced at Justin and Deanna then turned quickly around to talk to a customer on the other side of his booth. He didn't want to know.

"Not a bribe," Justin said, perfectly serious. "A gift. What would I be bribing you for anyway? I already got out of jail."

"For me to look the other way at whatever else you're up to."

Justin straightened the edge of the veil against Deanna's cheek, his fingers warm on her skin. "I'm giving you the veil because it looks pretty on you."

It did look nice. Too nice. Deanna shook off his touch and pulled the fabric from her head again, but she balled the silk in her hand and didn't return it to the vendor.

Justin had already started to walk away. Deanna hastened after him, swearing under her breath. Anyone who believed Shareem weren't masters of manipulation hadn't met Justin.

He didn't go far. She caught up to him when he stopped at a coffee vendor's and ordered two cups of thick Bor Nargan coffee, which was grown in the northern mountains. People came from planets far, far away to get Bor Nargan coffee.

A rare open space beyond the coffee vendor's stall provided tables. Justin deftly took one from three workers who were leaving and set down a coffee for Deanna. He waited for her to sit first at the high table, but she really shouldn't sit down in public with him. She was the patroller, he the former prisoner.

But he'd stand there all day waiting, she realized, so she plopped into a seat.

She snatched up the coffee and drank, closing her eyes at the taste of the deep, rich brew. He'd bought the top of the line—at least, as top of the line as you could get in Pas City.

Deanna opened her eyes to find Justin sitting across the table from her. He kept his gaze on her while he took a sip from his own cup.

He didn't do anything radical with that sip—he simply drank the coffee. But the way he drank it . . . He took it lovingly into his mouth, closing his eyes while he savored the taste. His throat moved in a slow swallow, then he slid his tongue over his lips to catch any lingering drop.

Deanna's knees went weak, something hot stabbing the space between her legs. The man couldn't do anything without being over-the-top sensual.

He opened his eyes and carefully set down his cup. "Wear the veil."

She shook her head. "I can't. Not while I'm in uniform."

Justin moved his gaze to her coverall where it hugged her bosom. "Patrollers live in those uniforms. You should have said, *not while I'm on duty.* Are you?"

Deanna rolled her cup between her palms. "No."

"Why not?"

She didn't want to tell him. Being a patroller was Deanna's life. She'd been a patroller since she'd graduated from the academy, had moved up the chain with ease. She stood to be promoted soon.

Until Justin.

She clutched the cup while humiliation crawled through her. "This morning, I was told to take a leave of absence."

She waited for Justin's laugh, his satisfied glee, but he watched her without changing expression. "I thought they were only holding up your promotion."

"Today they decided I should take a few days off while they look into my performance and decide what to do."

"Fucking patrollers," Justin growled.

Deanna shrugged, shoulders shaking a little. "It's procedure. I screwed up."

"Don't justify it. The arrest was legit, and we both know it."

"They're embarrassed and looking for someone to blame. I guess Brianne d'Aroth's word carries a lot of weight."

To her surprise, Justin grinned in true mirth. "I believe it. I haven't known Bree long, but I can see that she gets her own way. She'd have to have that kind of moxie, to put up with Aiden and Ky."

"Moxie? What does that mean?"

"Word I picked up on Sirius. Means she has balls, guts, lots of determination." Justin leaned forward. "You do too, I'm thinking. Wear the veil. To hell with them."

She shouldn't. Deanna had learned from day one, *Respect the uniform.*

Patrollers never went off duty, not really. They kept their eye out for crime every minute they were awake. Deanna had an alarm next to her bed wired straight from the stationhouse so they could wake her whenever she was needed.

Patrollers kept the streets safe for citizens of Bor Narga. Off-worlders came here by the ton, beings from all over the galaxy, and not all of them respected Bor Nargan laws. Deanna had stood between off-world rioters and the homes of Bor Nargans more than once, fought a slaver hand-to-hand when he was getting ready to abscond with two children. She'd hauled his sorry ass to her cells and got him transported to a maximum security station to await trial. Which he'd lost. Served him right. Scumbag.

Deanna *was* her uniform. She'd given her life to
the patrollers, believed in what they stood for.

And they'd cold-shouldered her the minute
she'd made a mistake. Which hadn't been a mistake.
Her prisoner was admitting his guilt.

But it didn't count, because all the ruling family
had to do was say a word, and it was Deanna who
paid.

Deanna shook out the veil with an angry jerk,
laid it over her head and wrapped the ends around
her throat.

Justin smiled. "Mmm. Beautiful."

"The silk is nice." Nicer than anything she
owned.

"I meant *you* are beautiful. Take the compliment,
Deanna."

When he said it in that velvet voice, Deanna
wanted to believe it.

"Tell me what you were researching at the
library," she said.

He shook his head. "Damn, you're like a dog
with a bone."

"I always get my prisoner."

"I bet you do. How about, instead of talking
about me, we talk about you. Who are you Deanna
Surrell? Why are you a patroller?"

Easy to answer, if he wanted to play this game.
"It's what I always wanted to do."

"What, your mother gave you a pistol and a
badge when you were five, and you went around the
house arresting your dolls?"

She flushed. "Yes, actually. Something like that. But I'd wanted to be a patroller before that. My mother was just humoring me." Deanna had wanted her mother to be so proud. And her mother was, the rare times she could communicate.

Justin took another sip of coffee, another lesson in sensuality. "So you went to the academy," he said. "Were you top of the class?"

"No." But pretty damn good. "I won a marksmanship medal."

"Shit, no wonder you got me. If you'd been shooting with a regular gun, I'd be dead."

"You would be," Deanna said. "But I'm not a killer. I subdue the target but keep him alive."

"And drag him to the cells to interrogate him."

"And make sure he's well cared for in my custody. Wounds healed, nutrition taken care of, no abuse. Some of the patrollers can be . . ."

Deanna closed her mouth over the criticism. Fine to complain within the division, bad to spill about it to a civilian, especially a Shareem.

"Yeah, I know how the patrollers can be," Justin said. "What makes you such a sweetie?"

"I'm not. I do my job."

He grinned. "So all Bor Nargans can rest easy in their beds?"

"Patrollers swear to protect and defend the ordinary citizens of Bor Narga. That's what I do."

"From the big, bad Shareem?"

"If necessary. What were you doing up on the Vistara, Justin?"

Justin raised his hands, still grinning, but his gaze became wary. "I told you, love. What Shareem do."

"Which is what, exactly?"

"The usual. Look it up."

"I'm asking *you*. No evasions and half-truths. I want to know, in every detail, why you decided to go to the Vistara two mornings ago and what you intended to do there."

His smile vanished. "If I tell you, then what? You arrest me again?"

"I don't have the power to arrest you at the moment." Deanna's fingers curled on the table. "But if you were breaking the law, or intending to, you don't get to go free."

"What if I promise you no laws would have been broken?"

"In that case, you can tell me what you were going to do."

Justin turned his head to study the nearby stalls overflowing with spices and exotic fruits. Deanna saw in his eyes, in the moment before he turned away, a flash of deep pain.

"I'll think about it," he said.

"I'm a patroller. I'm questioning you. You have to answer me."

When Justin turned back, the pain she'd glimpsed had vanished, and she wondered whether she'd imagined it.

"You were given a leave of absence," he said. "So you're a civvy right now, same as me."

"Justin," she said in exasperation.

He leaned forward, his gaze all for her. "I like it when you say my name like that. Your face gets all soft, and you lose the stick up your ass. It's like you want to talk to *me*."

"I do want to talk to you. Why won't you *tell* me?"

"Because you want to know so bad." He smiled again, a hot, melting smile. "I'm level two, sweetie. I tease, I drive you crazy, you beg for me, and I give you what I know you want."

When he said *beg for me*, Deanna had a sudden vision of herself on her knees, her hands bound together by her new silk veil, she asking Justin to do whatever he liked with her.

She also remembered her dream of him tied up on the chair, ropes snaking around his aroused cock while he instructed her to get undressed. She squirmed in her seat.

"Like that," Justin said in a low, warm voice.

Deanna hopped down from her stool. "Cease."

"I'm not doing anything. I'm drinking coffee."

"Yes, you are. You're *Shareem*-ing me."

Justin burst out laughing, a true laugh, not a teasing one. Passing women glanced over and smiled.

"Shareem-ing you. I have to remember that one."

Deanna's face went hot. "You know what I mean. What you do with your smiles, and your sips of coffee, and touching me with your pheromones."

"I swear to you, baby, I'm keeping my pheromones to myself. You, on the other hand, are sending out signals like crazy."

"I am not."

"Yes, you are. You're thinking about something that involves me, and it's making you want me."

"You are an arrogant, son of a . . . *vat*. I do not want you."

"Yes, you do. I'm right, aren't I?"

He was, and she'd never admit it.

"Go home, and stay there," Deanna said swiftly. "If I catch you going to the Vistara again, I swear to the gods I'll shoot you in the ass, and I won't use a stun gun this time." The veil brushed her cheek as she gesticulated, and she started to slide it off. "And take this back. I don't want it."

Justin's hands stilled hers. "Yes, you do." He smoothed the veil back into place, and Deanna stood, frozen, while his fingers brushed her cheek. "You deserve it for putting up with me."

His touch was warm. Deanna found it difficult to breath, while at the same time her heart pounded sickeningly hard. She wanted to turn her head and lick the side of his thumb, maybe take his fingertip into her mouth.

Justin brushed her cheek again, his gaze holding hers. Deanna's body was warm, pliant, the secret wanting she tried to banish twining her in an impossible grip.

The moment hung while the colors, scents, and sounds of the marketplace whirled around and became a background blur.

Justin skimmed his hand down her arm and closed his strong fingers around hers. "Walk me home."

It was not a command, not a suggestion, and he didn't plead. He simply said it.

Deanna twitched her hand from his, but she nodded. Justin flashed another smile at her, one of the amazing ones that lit up his face and made her want to collapse at his feet.

Side by side, they left the marketplace, back to the searing hot streets of Pas City.

Justin's flat was next to the bar run by the woman called Judith. Two Shareem stood in the bar's open doorway, a dark-haired one with massive muscles next to a tall blond Shareem with a face of perfect masculine beauty.

The dark man took one look at Deanna, scowled at her, and faded back into the bar, but the blond man eyed her with interest.

Justin ignored the two Shareem completely as he palmed open his door and pulled Deanna inside. The door slammed closed behind her, the lights coming on.

"Now stay here," Deanna started to say.

Justin backed her against the wall. "You think I can let you go yet? With you looking so beautiful?"

Before Deanna could do more than gape, Justin cupped her face in his hands and pulled her up to him for a hard, hot kiss.

Chapter Five

Justin tasted the fire in her. Deanna was shaking, uncertain, but he scented her wanting, which filled him with elation he hadn't experienced in a long time. He'd had so much grief, and now he wanted a patroller who'd shot him in the ass.

He slanted his mouth over Deanna's, sweeping his tongue inside. He was Shareem—he couldn't simply kiss a woman and be done. He had to take her mouth, learn it, explore it.

As her body softened under his, Justin licked the corners of her lips, drew his tongue across her bottom lip, and teased beneath her tongue. She tasted of the coffee, the rich, heady coffee of Bor Narga. Plain and simple, but oh, so strong.

The veil hid the severe bun she insisted on and drew attention from the drab gray coverall. The red silk emphasized her dark eyes, the rich brown of her hair.

And it was damn sexy. This woman had his cock hard, and she was a patroller, for the gods' sakes.

If he seduced her, if he took her into his bedroom for a long and satisfying afternoon delight, would she leave him the hell alone? Or arrest him again?

No, she was off duty. Forced to take a leave of absence, because of him.

So she'd just call another patroller to come and arrest him.

Justin eased the kiss to a close but kept his hands curled around her face, thumbs caressing her skin.

"You are fucking with my head," he said softly.

"What?"

"You're beautiful, and I'm lonely." And horny. So far, Justin had been making do with his ever-vigilant hand, but that had to stop sometime. Shareem needed sex.

Braden had offered to fix him up with a woman or two to work it off, but Justin hadn't wanted to be well into a two-day binge and miss any window of opportunity to see his daughter.

Besides, he'd learned the difference between sex with love and sex for the sake of satiation. He preferred the love, though he knew he'd have to sate himself soon or explode.

But he was beginning to like this feisty little patroller. A day with her, teaching her everything she needed to know about Shareem . . .

Justin's level-two instincts knocked. He could lock her hands behind her, strip her bare, run slow fingers over her body, then kiss her, lick her, bite her, and show her that a little spanking between friends could be fun.

Deanna was ready, he could feel it in her. Her skin temperature was rising, face now a sweet pink. Her need was filling her, probably surprising her, and Justin had to talk fast.

"Tell you what," he said. "You let me teach you about Shareem—what we really are, not a bunch of crap in your database. Let me teach you, and maybe I'll tell you what I was doing up on the Vistara."

He let the lie come to his lips, without stirring up the pain and sweat that other Shareem went through.

Half-lie, actually. He wouldn't tell her about Sybellie, but he might help Deanna save her job— somehow. It was important to her.

Deanna leaned to him. Her lips parted, her breath touching his fingers, and her mouth started to form the word *Yes*.

"No," she said.

A hard, emphatic *No*.

Disappointment kicked him in the gut. He'd been looking forward to taking her by the wrists and tugging her with him into his bedroom. *Right now.*

Justin could still do it. He'd broken his programming. He didn't need her permission.

"No?" he asked softly.

"I'm not a whore, thank you very much. No *learning* about Shareem in exchange for anything."

Fair point. "All right. How about learning about Shareem for the hell of it?"

That stopped her. Deanna wanted it—everything about her screamed it. Her body was tight under his touch, nipples pearling against her coverall.

Deanna took a firm step away. "No."

She had to drag the word out, but the woman had guts. Not many females could resist a Shareem when they poured it on.

"No," she said again. Deanna managed to slide herself along the wall toward the door, though she couldn't look away from him.

Justin let her go. He could take her, sure. He could make her like it so much that she never told a soul and kept it her secret pleasure forever.

He could do anything he wanted, but Justin had the feeling that if he coerced her into it now, this would be their one and only time. As much as he could make her like it, Deanna would be ashamed, and she wouldn't be back for more.

But it hurt, oh, it hurt, to watch her go.

"Stay here," she said, her voice stronger the farther she made it from Justin. She touched the door controls. The door flung itself upward, as though it too was in haste to get her out of there. Hot air boiled in at them. "And stay the hell off the Vistara."

Deanna walked out. Almost ran out. She gave Justin one last look over her shoulder—her longing burning him as her veil glistened in the sunlight—then the door closed, and she was gone.

"Shit."

Justin ran his hands through his hair, his body sweating, though the cooler tried to staunch the heat. He was going to burn up and die.

He wanted to run after Deanna, haul her back in here, take her against the wall. To drown in her scent, to taste every inch of her—he *needed* it.

Damn her.

Justin collapsed to the sofa, scrubbing his hands through his hair, trying to stop the tingling all over his skin. He needed to release. Shareem genes were taking over, and he needed to release, *now, now, now.*

Oh, right, I broke my programming and can live like a normal human.

I'm Shareem, and I always will be.

It was time to see Sybellie. But Justin couldn't sneak to the Vistara and the coffeehouse where she met her friends when he was burning up like this. He'd never walk three feet with this hard-on.

Judith was next door, a woman who made no secret that she loved Shareem—four or five at a time when she could manage it.

But as she'd indicated when Justin had squeezed her ass the other day, she was holding off Shareem. She liked Mitch, Mitch had asked her to be exclusive, and who was Justin to come between a budding relationship?

Justin occasionally still joined Braden and Elisa for a little ménage fun, but right now he needed mindless fucking, and he didn't think Braden would stand back and let that happen. Neither would Elisa, and anyway Justin didn't want to use Elisa that way.

That left his handy hand.

He didn't have time to make it a formal ritual or even grab some lube. Justin ripped open his leggings, wrapped his hand around his hard and unhappy cock, and yanked.

* * * * *

Deanna didn't catch her breath until she was halfway down the street. The veil had sunblocking material woven into the silk, which shielded her from the worst of the sun, but her body was scalding from the inside out.

She still felt Justin's mouth on hers, his skilled kiss, his fingers gentle on her face. Her body was burning to its core, her need making her hotter than she'd ever been.

Even Deanna's dream about him hadn't gotten her this bothered. But that hadn't been real, and Justin's searing kiss had been. While she'd stood against him, taking the kiss, she'd wanted to grab his big hand, thrust it between her legs, and beg him to pleasure her.

When he'd offered to tell her what she wanted to know in exchange for teaching her, she'd nearly screamed *Yes!*

Deanna's hasty claim that she wouldn't make a whore of herself for him had been a huge lie. She'd wanted to. Justin made her want to. And when he'd suggested they do it for the fun of it . . .

Good thing she'd gotten herself out of there.

Deanna leaned against the wall in a nearby alley, trying to let the heat of the sun-baked brick restore her equilibrium. As she waited, she forced her common sense to return.

In spite of the way he wooed her today, Justin was still up to something. He'd returned to Bor Narga for a reason, and he'd gone to the Vistara for a reason, and that reason was costing Deanna her job, her career, and her life.

She damn well wanted to find out what that reason was. And she would—no letting him distract her with buying her gifts and promising her pleasure.

Deanna wasn't certain how long she stayed in the alley, watching and waiting, trying to calm down, but the sun moved higher, and plenty of people passed by.

She came alert when a sleek hovercar pulled up in front of Justin's door. The car was expensive, if Deanna were any judge, barely making any noise as it rocked on its cushion of air.

The car had a driver's compartment separate from the passenger's—the type of car its owner would never drive herself. A highborn woman lurked behind those tinted windows in the back, Deanna was certain, a chauffeur in the front.

After about five minutes, the door to Justin's apartment opened. Justin strolled out, cool and collected, his sunblocking robes pulled over his head and across the lower half of his face. The back passenger door opened quietly for him, and Justin climbed inside.

The door closed, and the car slid forward, heading straight for Deanna.

Deanna ducked back into the shadows of the alley. As soon as the car passed, she came out of hiding and followed.

The streets down here were full of people, slowing the hovercar, so Deanna easily kept up with it, and the driver didn't seem to be in a hurry. The car wove patiently through the pedestrian traffic and didn't pick up speed until it found a main thoroughfare. Deanna stepped back as the car turned the last corner and darted into the stream of traffic flowing uphill.

"Damn him," she said out loud, the vestiges of her longing washed away by anger.

The thoroughfare was the direct route to the Vistara, the hill upon which upper middleclass and aspiring upper-class women bought homes, raised children to be as snobbish as they were, and dreamed someday of moving on to the Serestine Quarter.

Growling in rage, Deanna sprinted back down the street, never minding the heat. She used her badge that she carried on duty or off to rush past the turnstile at the nearest station, and leapt onto the first train heading up to the Vistara.

Chapter Six

Justin barely made it. He stayed well under the shadows of the passage across the street from the coffeehouse, and looked over at the four girls at their usual table inside.

The other three young women were daughters of local well-off families, and they all went to the nearby university graduate school with Sybellie. Sybellie was studying techno-finance, he'd had Elisa look up. He was proud of how smart she was.

As Justin watched, Sybellie lifted her coffee to her lips then threw her head back and laughed at something one of her friends said.

She robbed him of breath every time he saw her. She looked much like her mother, Lillian, but Sybellie had also gotten Justin's genes, which had been engineered to produce strength, physical beauty, stamina, and robust health.

Sybellie glowed with beauty. Her hair was soft brown, her eyes brown—happily Lillian's dominant Bor Nargan gene had not betrayed Sybellie by giving her blue eyes. The young woman laughed readily, her pink cheeks matching the rose-colored veils she liked to wear.

In short, she was a twenty-something-year-old woman, happy with her friends, poised to take on life.

Justin had never met her and had never spoken to her. He could only stand here day after day and gaze at her, wishing like hell he could walk to her, take her hand, sit down next to her and say, "Hello, Sybellie. I'm your dad."

He never could. Shareem, in theory, weren't able to reproduce. But Justin had managed it with Lillian. A fluke, a lucky shot.

A beautiful lucky shot, there with her friends, so happy.

Someone punched him in the ass. No, not punched, shoved a pistol onto his right butt cheek.

"I told you what I'd do if I found you up here again."

Deanna had a bedroom voice even when she was threatening him. She was still wearing the silk veil too.

Justin turned abruptly, grabbed the wrist of the hand holding the pistol, and flattened Deanna to the wall.

"Shut up," he said in a low, fierce voice.

Deanna's eyes widened, but in fury, not fear. "Let go of me."

"Keep it down."

She struggled. "I yell once, and every patroller on the Vistara guns you down."

"That's why I need you to *shut up*."

"I'm not afraid of you."

"I don't give a shit. Don't say a word."

The door of the coffeehouse slid open, and the four girls came out, talking together. They pulled silken veils down to keep out the heat, but didn't stop their chatter, which they all seemed to be doing at once.

Justin did his best not to look. He tried not to turn his head, to not so much as move an eyeball.

But he couldn't help it. Sybellie tossed her veil around her throat, her clear voice touching Justin like a caress.

Deanna glared at him. "You're up here to watch them, aren't you? Aren't they a little young for you?"

"I wasn't watching them." Justin had gotten so good at lying.

She ignored him. "Are you stalking one of them? Was she who you were coming up here to meet? If she's underage, you are so screwed. Tell me, Justin. I'll find out anyway. Or was it all of them together?"

Justin pushed her harder into the wall. "You leave them the hell alone."

Deanna's eyes widened again, this time with a look of pain. "Oh, gods, Justin, you really are stalking them."

"No, I am not."

"Then why are you up here? Why are you risking your life?"

Justin let go of her, fear swirling through him. "All right, all right." He raised his hands, pretending to be cool, when his heart was pounding so hard he wanted to die. "It's true," he said quickly. "I'm a perv. I like young, soft flesh."

Deanna's eyes narrowed. "You're lying."

"Shareem can't lie."

"But you're doing it. Again."

Fuck.

Her pistol came up. It was a stun pistol only, but she could drag him anywhere if she knocked him out.

"You are going to tell me every word of what's going on," she said. "Or I'll arrest you again, and I don't care how many d'Aroths gang up on me to get you out."

"Fine." Justin reached into his robes. Deanna's trigger finger tightened until Justin pulled out his handheld. "I'll call my ride. It's more comfortable than a patrol car."

"Why not watch from the car, then, where I couldn't find you or shoot you?"

Justin pushed buttons that summoned the chauffeur. "You wouldn't understand."

Bor Nargan glass tended to be very thick and full of shielding. Looking through the shielded glass of Brianne's car to the heavy windows of the coffeehouse rendered the coffeehouse's windows an almost opaque gray. If he stayed in the car, he wouldn't get a clear view of Sybellie.

The car slid to a silent halt at the other end of the alley. Justin grabbed Deanna's hand and towed her along with him toward it.

The car's back door slid open. Justin all but shoved Deanna inside and climbed in behind her, dropping onto the seat with her before the door closed again.

The chauffeur turned and looked at them through the window of his compartment. Deanna's gun was obvious, but Justin shook his head.

"It's all right," he said through the speaker.

The chauffeur, used to Shareem by now, turned away and darkened the window between passenger and driver compartments.

The car was a bubble of privacy and luxury. Cushions softer than any bed Justin had owned cradled his backside. The air was cooled and lightly scented with the odor of meadow flowers. Justin had walked across real meadows on Sirius, and knew that they smelled of mud, decayed grass, and the last passing cow. But none of that would do for the highborn ladies on Bor Narga.

"How did you afford this?" Deanna asked, looking around in wonder.

"I didn't. It's a friend's. She loaned it to me for the afternoon."

"What friend?"

"Brianne d'Aroth."

Deanna made a noise of exasperation. "I might have known. She's been very helpful, hasn't she? Is she one of your . . . clients?"

"No," Justin said with emphasis. "She's just a friend."

"Why should I believe anything you say?"

"Why are you trying to make my life hell?" Justin countered.

They faced each other, Deanna breathing hard, red-faced, and still sexy.

"Why did you come back to Bor Narga?" Deanna asked.

"Why is it any of your damned business?"

"Because it's my job to protect women from people like you!" Her voice rang in the small compartment.

"Oh, right, to protect the women who make so many rules that my friends and I can barely exist? The same women who hire us in secret to make them orgasm all night? You're protecting them from *me*?"

"You didn't have to come back here," Deanna said hotly. "You lived on Sirius, for the gods' sake. You left there to come back to this hellhole. You're up to something. I need to know what."

"Nothing that's going to hurt you or the precious women you're protecting."

"How the hell can I know that?" Deanna shouted. "Shareem aren't supposed to lie, but you're doing it. Shareem can't touch a woman without her permission, but you grabbed me and shoved me around without a flicker of pain. Has someone been messing with you inside? Did they break your programming? Who was it, and what does it have to do with those girls?"

"*I* broke it." Justin grabbed her wrist again without mitigating his strength and twisted the stun gun from her hand. "I broke my programming myself. It has nothing to do with anyone on Bor Narga. With more than twenty years on Sirius without the stupid inoculations, I had plenty of time to practice."

Deanna stared, openmouthed, as he clicked on the stun gun's safety and tossed the gun to the other side of the car. "I could have you terminated for doing that."

"Fine. Then do it." Justin shoved his handheld at her. "Call your patrollers. Arrest me. Terminate me. Hell, I don't care anymore."

He did care, but Deanna was right. He shouldn't have come back to Bor Narga. But after Shela had died, his craving to see Sybellie wouldn't leave him alone.

Now he realized his selfishness. Deanna wasn't stupid. If she figured out what was going on, if she reported it, he might as well have killed his own daughter.

Deanna took the handheld, but she rested it between her fingertips and didn't turn it on. "I don't want you terminated, Justin." Her voice was low, that bedroom silkiness again. "I told you that when you were in the cell. I would have helped you out of there, without you having to bother Brianne d'Aroth. Why didn't you believe me?"

"You're a patroller."

"You're a Shareem."

She continued to rotate the handheld between her fingers, not making any move to use it.

"That means we're always enemies?" he asked her.

Deanna's eyes were soft. "I don't want us to be."

Justin didn't want them to be either. Not enemies. In different circumstances he'd be happy to get to know this lady. She had beauty, strength, and grit, as the plain, hardworking folks on Sirius liked to say.

As Deanna continued to turn the handheld, Justin scooped the veil back from her face. He caressed the corners of her mouth with his thumbs, parting her lips, studying the red, moist heat of her mouth.

Justin leaned closer, her breath on his skin as soft as the silk veil. Her hands came up to rest against his chest, the corner of the handheld pressing his tunic.

Justin parted her lips a little more before he slanted his mouth across hers.

He tasted the heat of her as he stroked his tongue inside her, felt the pulse pounding in her throat as he slid his fingers down her neck.

Deanna opened her lips to his, trying to imitate what he did. The flicker of her tongue was erotic as hell, making his already hard cock that much more rigid.

Justin slid his knee between her thighs, liking the
tight coverall that let him feel every part of her. She
gasped as he pressed her legs open, then her eyes
softened as he stroked his thigh against her pussy.

Her little noise of surrender made his Shareem
needs kick in. Justin looped his hand around her
wrists, holding them locked together while he
pushed her down to the seat.

She squirmed under him, but Justin held her
firmly, continuing to lick and stroke her mouth. His
questing fingers found the fastening of her coverall,
and he jerked the coverall open from neck to waist.

Beneath it, Deanna wore an almost sheer tunic,
the rosy buds of her nipples displayed against the
fabric. Justin held her down while he tongued one
nipple through the tunic, loving how it rose and
tightened against his lips. Deanna arched up to him
as Justin closed his mouth over her breast and
suckled.

He could have her now, holding her down on
the soft cushion of the seat. He could tear the silk
open and feast on her bare flesh, licking his way
down to her pussy, which he could scent was wet
and open for him.

She'd taste good, her hot spice flavoring the bare
flower of her pussy, the hard berry of her clit. Then
he'd have the coverall off, and he'd thrust into her,
sating the need that was burning him up.

The driver couldn't see—he'd cut off sound and
sight to give his passengers privacy. The man was
used to driving Brianne with Aiden and Ky. He'd

probably learned a long time ago that it was best not to know what went on in his back seat.

Justin's imagination flicked briefly to Aiden and Ky, two hard-bodied Shareem sandwiching pretty Brianne, in this compartment, pheromones thick, and his libido snapped tighter. Justin liked a bit of voyeurism now and again to whet his appetite — these days, he didn't have much more than that.

But the picture quickly dissolved. He wanted it to be just him and just Deanna, for them to find their deepest pleasure alone together.

Justin kissed his way up to her throat. "Hire me," he whispered.

"What?"

"Hire me." He raised his head. "Like I offered before, let me show you what being with a Shareem can be."

Deanna gave him a little smile, her eyes languid. "You mean, this isn't it?"

"No." Not by a long way. He wanted to discover every single one of her desires and feed them to her. "Hire me, and I'll give you a night you'll never forget."

From the heat blossoming in her eyes, she wanted it. She wanted him. Her body gave off desire in waves, the female scent of her kicking Justin's hard-on into high gear.

Her eagerness died. "I can't."

No, no, sweetheart, don't say no. "Yes, you can."

Deanna shook her head. "I don't want it to be like that."

Neither did Justin. He wanted her to be with him because she wanted him, nothing more.

On Sirius, selling sexual favors had been illegal. Sex between two consenting adult beings—human, alien, cyborg, same sex, same whatever—was fine, but no using sex as a commodity. Almost the opposite of Bor Narga, where physical sex was taboo, but ladies secretly hired Shareem for forbidden pleasure.

Justin traced her cheek. "Here's what I want you to do. Go home. Get plenty of rest. Then come back and find me. I'll give you a night. Just you and me, no strings, no contracts. Just you and me," he repeated, kissing her. "Understand?"

"Justin, I'm a patroller."

"On leave of absence. Leave the uniform at home. We'll be Justin and Deanna, not patroller and Shareem, not anybody but us."

The car slowed and stopped, and Justin knew they'd reached his apartment. "All right?" he asked, not moving.

Deanna's breath came fast, her chest rising to his. "I'll think about it."

"Think until dark. Then come to me."

"I said, I'll *think* about it."

Feisty sweetheart. "Fine." Justin sat up, gently pulled her coverall together and fastened it, then turned on the speaker to the chauffeur. "Take the lady wherever she wants to go."

"Got it," the chauffeur answered.

The door next to Justin slid open, revealing the dusty street and Justin's front door.

Justin pulled Deanna up for one last kiss, then he extricated himself from the car and signaled for the driver to go. He stepped back and made himself not give in to his impulse to dive back into the car and ravish Deanna all the way home.

The car sped off, spewing dust all over Justin while he stood in the street and watched them go.

* * * * *

Justin knew he'd never last until Deanna came back—*if* she came back. She was the kind of woman who'd talk herself out of giving in to her desires. Justin might have to chase her a little harder, but he didn't mind the chase. In fact, he looked forward to it.

But right now, his body was hot, his cock pounding hard again. His choices for release were to spend more time with his hand, to get falling down drunk, or to work it off.

He didn't want to be falling down drunk or hung over if Deanna returned, and his hand wasn't the funnest date, so he decided to work it off.

Judith, the sweetie, had rented out a small warehouse and turned it into Shareem paradise. The place contained baths and showers, a private place to hang out and be with Shareem friends, and a dungeon-like room underneath where Shareem could bring their more adventurous ladies.

The enormous pool in the bath area had one mirrored wall, behind which women could sit and watch Shareem cavort, if cavorting Shareem was their thing.

Usually the pool was for Shareem alone, but today a lady was there—Jeanne, the lover of Eland. They were in the water together, both naked, Jeanne with legs wrapped around Eland while Eland cradled her hips in his hands. They never minded who watched whatever they did, those crazy kids.

Jeanne had been a factory worker who'd met Eland right after DNAmo shut down. She'd protected him from the patrollers who were hunting Shareem to terminate them, and Eland and Jeanne had hit it off.

When the termination order for all Shareem had been lifted, Eland and Jeanne had stayed together. They sometimes brought in other partners, male or female, for fun, but the two had formed a permanent bond.

Watching the two now in the water together, gazing into each other's eyes, gave Justin a lonely feeling. He was glad for them, but their happiness underscored the emptiness inside him.

"Get a room," Justin said jokingly as he stripped to the skin and splashed his way into the pool.

Chapter Seven

"We did," Eland rumbled. "We're relaxing."

Eland was big, even for a Shareem. A level three, he had muscles like a heavyweight wrestler.

Justin swam a lap, liking that the water was cool today, refreshing after the heat. Water cascaded into the pool from a stone spout high in a wall, and Justin came up under the waterfall.

"You're displacing half the pool with that cock," Eland said. "If you're going to blow in here, tell me so I can get out first."

"That's why I'm under the cold shower, idiot," Justin said. "Trying to deflate."

Jeanne sent him a smile. "We can help you, you know." She wriggled her tongue to let him know her mouth was available, as long as Eland was there to watch her use it.

But Justin wanted *Deanna's* mouth. Her red-lipped, soft mouth that turned up into such a cute smile.

Shit, why did he have to think of that? She wouldn't come to him tonight, and he'd have this erection forever.

"Thanks, but I'll swim it off." Justin tried to sound nonchalant, but his voice cracked.

Jeanne laughed at him. "I'm the wrong lady, am I? Uh-oh."

Justin snaked his hand under the water and squeezed his cock. *Calm down, dry up, go on vacation,* he told it.

It wasn't listening. Okay, change the subject.

He swam over to Eland and Jeanne, who watched him approach without much curiosity. When Justin was close enough that his words wouldn't carry to anyone who happened to be behind the mirrors, he asked, "Jeanne, any word?"

Jeanne glanced at the wall and also lowered her voice. "I might know someone who used to know her. A friend of mine said she knew a woman named Lillian who she *thinks* once worked at DNAmo."

Justin's heart beat faster. "Is this friend still in touch with her?"

"She hasn't seen Lillian for years now, she says. They'd been close friends, but Lillian moved from Pas City and never kept in touch."

Too much to hope for. "Can I talk to this friend?" Maybe she'd know enough about Lillian to give Justin a lead on where she might have gone.

"Sure," Jeanne said. "I'll set it up." She cocked Justin a look. "Sure you're not up for a little threesome action?"

"Not today, honey. I have a cock-ache."

Jeanne only shrugged. Eland gave Justin a look of sympathy, but one that told him he was an idiot for passing up the chance for sex.

Last week, Justin might have taken them up on it and gotten some heat out of his system. After meeting Deanna—not as appealing. Sex with friends was not what he wanted right now.

I have to be crazy. I'm looking for something deeper with a patroller.

Justin took himself out of the pool and hit the showers, setting the water temperature to freezing. He still needed his hand to finally release, so he could walk home without a big stick hanging between his legs.

He really needed a better life.

* * * * *

Deanna was home an hour before she stopped shaking. She hadn't even been able to enjoy the ride in the luxurious car, something she'd probably never have the chance to do again.

She still felt Justin's mouth on hers, robbing her of breath, his big body pressing her into the seat. He'd been heavy, too strong to fight, not that she'd wanted to fight.

Mouth on her nipple, tongue bringing it to life, making it his, as he'd stroked between her legs with his thigh. He'd been hard and ready, the ridge of his cock against her unbelievably huge.

To feel that going into her would be . . . Deanna had no idea. She had no context.

Her shaking finally stopped when her mother's companion, Reda, brought her mother home from the rehab center. Reda shook her head when Deanna looked a question, which told Deanna that her mother was having one of her bad days.

Deanna hugged her mother though the woman sat straight and unresponsive in her chair. Her eyes were focused on nothing as Reda combed out her silver and black hair.

The disorder that had afflicted Deanna's mother was technological, not physiological. Kayla Surrell had been on a layover in a space station and wandered by accident into an area that had been closed off for radiation leak repairs. She'd gotten dosed with some complicated chemical that Deanna still didn't understand, which had at first paralyzed her.

Kayla had survived by good luck alone — someone had spotted her and dragged her out into good air — but she'd never spoken again. The chemicals had tangled up her nervous system, and now, though she still had most of her motor functions, she did not respond to stimulus much of the time.

Some days, Kayla would almost respond, and Deanna would grow hopeful that her mother was getting better. Then she'd relapse into nothingness and have to have her every bodily need met by Reda and Deanna.

Deanna kissed her mother good night and let Reda put her to bed, though it was still early afternoon.

Justin had asked Deanna to return tonight, to be with him.

So, so tempting. Deanna would love one evening to forget everything, to feast her senses in a man like Justin, to *feel* something.

But she couldn't afford to let him bamboozle her. Her mother was why Deanna couldn't lose her job.

Deanna fixed a bite of late lunch in the kitchen and shut herself into her room with her computer. She had a pretty high clearance in the computer databases of Bor Narga, even on a leave of absence, and she was going to learn everything she could about Justin.

Not long later, Justin's case files from DNAmo opened like flowers under her fingertips. These records had been sealed, but now that more than twenty years had passed, access had been granted to those with the right clearance. A Patroller First Class, the highest level of the uniformed patrollers, had the right clearance.

Deanna went through the records, reading every word.

The notes on Justin indicated he hadn't given the researchers at DNAmo too much trouble. He'd stoically taken the researchers' experiments every day, experiments that had involved a lot of sex.

The first mention of any trouble was about a worker called K-48.

K-designated workers, colloquially referred to as "guinea pigs," were women hired by DNAmo to participate in sex experiments with the Shareem. The experiments were designed to find out what Shareem would do and how much they could be controlled under certain sets of circumstances—basically discovering what a level one would do, how far a level two would go, how rough a level three might get before his programming stopped him.

Justin performed as a perfect level two, the notes said, but his behavior toward K-48 was troubling.

Justin and K-48 talk to each other during the experiments, but we can't hear what they say. When asked what he is telling her, Justin refuses to answer, even when he is punished. We have no means of compelling K-48 to speak because of the privacy clause in her contract.

A later note said: *K-48 and the subject Justin were confined alone together for a seven-day period. During that time, Justin used every method he'd been taught on her and never seemed to run out of stamina: He let K-48 rest when she needed to, but he has a most unusual ability to work continuously.*

More entries about Justin's progress, much of it in medical-speak, with no mention of K-48, followed. Finally Deanna found another reference.

Justin's obsession with K-48 has reached an alarming level. He refused to participate in the day's experiments and demanded to know where she was and what happened to her. When told we couldn't convey that information, he turned violent and had to be confined.

The director agreed we could bring back K-48 to see what effect it had on him. K-48 appeared to be quite pleased to see Justin, and when left alone, they held on to each other for a long time. We became aware then that they were speaking rapidly, but we couldn't hear what was said, and we removed her.

I and the director conclude that the Shareem has formed an attachment to K-48. Because Shareem are to be programmed to form no attachments to their clients whatsoever, recommend immediate transfer of K-48 to another section.

A final note on K-48 said, *The Shareem Justin reacted violently when he was told that K-48 had been transferred and he'd not be allowed to see her again. He demanded assurances that she was all right and not harmed. Even after we gave him that, he was surly and uncooperative and had to be injected to calm him down.*

End of references to K-48. Apparently, Justin had gone back to being a compliant Shareem — either that or the researchers hadn't bothered bother to record any more of his reaction to the absence of K-48.

A few weeks later, Justin was sold to an off-world woman, packed up, and transported to Sirius, never to be seen on Bor Narga until a few months ago.

What about K-48? Deanna skimmed through the database until she found her.

Her records had been sealed for privacy, but again, Deanna's clearance and the requisite time having passed opened them.

K-48's image popped up on Deanna's holoscreen. A pretty young woman, sturdy of build, typical of the lower-class women of Pas City.

Her records contained a statement from her that she'd signed up for the program because of the high payment offered. She'd been paired only with Justin for the experiments, because she'd requested that she not be put with more than one Shareem at a time.

No details about the experiments were listed in her records, but a note said she'd been transferred to the level-one section the morning after the suggestion that she be moved had been put into Justin's file.

The day after K-48 was transferred, she terminated her contract and quit the program. Interesting.

K-48's name was Lillian Passan, a working-class woman from a working-class family in Pas City. She'd worked at DNAmo for a total of six months.

Deanna moved the DNAmo records to the background and did a general search on Lillian Passan. She easily found Lillian's birth records, her school records, her job history, and the record of her signing up for DNAmo. DNAmo had done background checks on their test subjects, so Lillian's entire life was now open to Deanna.

Not much to it. After Lillian had quit DNAmo, she'd moved back in with her parents. There, the information ended. No more jobs, no moves, no trips off planet. Nothing. She'd stayed home with her parents, and that was it.

Deanna keyed in the address of Lillian's family's apartment. No Passans living there now. A Rose Passan and a Samuel Passan who'd leased the apartment fifteen years ago were listed as deceased — Lillian's parents.

But no Lillian. Deanna did more searches on Lillian but found nothing.

She sat back, staring at the small holographic woman turning slowly on her console. If Deanna wanted an explanation of why Justin had returned to Bor Narga, this was it. His lifemate on Sirius had died, and he'd returned to find Lillian.

A little pain burned in Deanna's heart. She thought of Justin's lips on hers, he pushing her back onto the seat, his kiss one of desperate hunger. She thought of what he'd whispered to her in his apartment, *You are beautiful, and I'm lonely.*

He wanted her to go to him tonight.

But he'd returned to Bor Narga to find the woman with whom he'd formed an attachment at DNAmo.

Puzzling that Lillian had simply disappeared. No one on Bor Narga could do anything without a string of records following them.

And why had Justin been looking for her on the Vistara? His frequent trips there, despite all the warnings, made sense in the context of a continuous search for Lillian.

Deanna looked through records for the Vistara — for all of Bor Narga — and found no one named Lillian living on the Vistara or working for someone there.

Lillian could have changed her name, but there should be a record of that too. Such a thing could be done secretly, of course, in theory. Perhaps Lillian had known someone who could help her disappear.

But why? By all accounts, Lillian had been a hard worker, a decent student, and a law-abiding citizen who was fond of her parents. She'd never been arrested, warned, or even looked at by the patrollers.

Deanna fanned out her search to cover the few years between Lillian quitting DNAmo to shortly after her parents' deaths. She broadened the search to include any new person popping up from nowhere during that time, or any incident involving an unknown woman of the right age.

Three deaths of unidentified persons had been recorded in that window of time, but two of those had been off-world human males and one an alien. It was unusual when even DNA couldn't identify a body, but it was known to happen if off-world records were spotty.

There were a few births with "mother unknown" attached, which Deanna at first ignored, until a date caught her attention.

She'd seen a similar date somewhere on her search. After a moment's thought, she keyed open Justin's DNAmo records again.

There it was, the date of Lillian's transfer. No, it was not the same date as the birth—same day, same year, but different month.

Deanna's breath caught, her entire body squeezing until she thought she'd choke.

Lillian Passan had finished her seven-day confinement experiment with Justin almost nine months to the day that a girl had been born to an anonymous mother in a backstreet clinic.

It could mean nothing. Coincidence. Bor Narga had a large population, and many children had been born that day, even in backstreet clinics in Pas City.

But only one had been born to an unknown woman of the same age as Lillian. A daughter. The girl who'd been born that day would now be about twenty-four years old.

Deanna's thoughts flashed back to Justin standing in the alley on the Vistara, gazing across the street with longing at the group of four young women in the coffeehouse. Each of the girls had been about that age.

No. No. It was impossible. Shareem couldn't father children. All the science in the DNAmo records said so. They were programmed not to, that programming backed up with sterility injections.

But the evidence was there for anyone who wanted to take time to look and think.

Justin had grown too fond of a test subject, Lillian had quit right after DNAmo removed her from Justin's reach, and she'd gone home to live quietly with her parents. Justin had returned to Bor Narga after his lifemate passed. He went to the Vistara and continued going even when he knew such an action could get him terminated. He went there to stand and gaze across the street at a young woman in a coffeehouse.

His daughter.

Deanna sat back in her chair, closed her eyes, and pressed her hands to her face.

* * * * *

Justin groaned. He was wet from his about fourth freezing shower but not cold—no one was ever cold on Bor Narga. He leaned, naked, against the wall in his living room, his hand around his needy cock.

He couldn't stop thinking about Deanna. She with that veil framing her face, her body moving under his on the seat of the car, the amazing taste of her.

She'd said she'd think about coming back.

Crap, she wasn't coming back. Justin was dreaming to think she was. His trip to the baths hadn't helped, and the cold shower he'd just finished in his own bathroom hadn't helped either.

The only thing that would help was Deanna.

Next best thing—fantasizing about her while he stroked himself.

Justin at least had the chance to use lube this time. His cock was slick under his fingers, the shaft hard and hot, the tip so sensitive a moan escaped him every time he touched it.

He leaned his head on the wall and imagined Deanna's smaller, softer hand gripping him, or better still, her red-lipped mouth closing around him, her tongue tickling the underside.

Oh, yeah. That's it, baby. Suck me. Harder. Harder. Pleeease!

A faint buzzing tapped at his senses, but he could barely hear it over the roaring in his head. It sounded again, and then his door shot upward, sending in dying afternoon light, and Deanna herself.

Chapter Eight

Deanna wasn't wearing the veil, Justin saw before the door slammed shut behind her.

She stopped and stared at him, eyes widening as she took in his naked body, his cock sliding between his fist, his parted legs. Whatever she'd been about to say died on her lips.

Justin smiled a little as he squeezed his hand harder around his cock.

"Hey, sexy," he said.

Deanna's mouth closed, but her gaze fell to his cock and stayed there. Justin stroked it again, opening his fingers to show her how hard he was for her.

"Guess what I'm thinking about?" he asked.

She swallowed. "Sex."

"You." Justin skimmed his hand to the base of his cock again. "I was waiting for you, thinking about you and what I wanted to do to you. I was remembering your beautiful breast in my mouth. I shouldn't have done that."

"No, you shouldn't have," Deanna said. "I'm a patroller—"

"I meant I shouldn't have thought about it. Look what it did to me."

Justin squeezed himself again. Gods, she was gorgeous, with her bedroom eyes and her sultry body, even if her hair was scraped back again into that hard knot.

He couldn't think anymore. He could only see her, scent her pheromones, feel her desire all the way across the room.

"Help me," he said. "Please."

Deanna wet her lips, making them redder, and sending his fantasies soaring. "I don't know how."

"Come here. I'll show you." Justin reached his free hand out for her, hoping he could stop himself from begging too hard. If he had to achieve the release by himself, he'd just get hard again. Shareem stamina was a bitch.

Deanna walked to him. Sweet lady. Justin took her hand when she reached him, and carefully wrapped it around his cock.

"Like this." He kept his hand around hers and pulled them together down the shaft.

He almost came right away. But no, his strength held it back, the science beaten into him letting him keep it hard for his lady.

Deanna looked up at him as she glided her hand under his. Her eyes were so dark and beautiful he couldn't stop the next groan. He wrapped his arm around her waist, pulled her against him, and let go so she could stroke him alone.

Deanna had a hard time catching her breath. Justin's body against her side was strong, hard, and still wet from a shower. He leaned back against the wall, one fist clenched at his side, the other hand resting on Deanna's waist. His cock in her hand felt . . . wonderful.

The oil or whatever he'd put on it made it slick, so Deanna easily slid her hand up its length. The heat was incredible. His tip was a little bit softer than the rest, flesh giving beneath her fingers.

Back and forth she took her hand, then once she became more confident, she started twisting and pulling. She wasn't sure why she wanted to do that, she just did.

Justin's hips began to rock, which pushed his cock through her closed hand. The more she twisted and pulled, the faster he thrust.

"That's it," he whispered. "Gods, Deanna, you are beautiful."

She'd never thought so. But *he* was beautiful. His naked male flesh was browned from working in the sun on Sirius, and the body she rested against was so hard with muscle she didn't feel a slackness anywhere.

His chest rose and fell with his swift breath, his lower abdomen shiny from where the lubrication he'd put around his cock had smeared on his skin.

The strength of him was amazing, but his large, work-worn hand on her waist was gentleness itself.

The friction from stroking him made Deanna's palm hot, but she didn't want to stop. She brushed her thumb over his tip, liking the slightly rubbery feel of it contrasted with his iron-hard shaft. She liked caressing beneath the tip as well, because that made him make more noises of pleasure.

Justin's strong fingers closed around her wrist. His head was back against the wall, eyes closed, lips parted in ecstasy.

"I'm coming," he whispered, then it became a throaty rumble. "Gods am I ever coming."

She felt the pulses begin, Justin's body moving, and suddenly, his male seed jetted out all over her hand. Ropes of come snaked to the floor and his legs, Justin putting his clean hand over his face while he let out a heartfelt moan.

Then it was over. Justin's face went grim as he furrowed Deanna's hair with firm fingers, pulled her head back, and kissed her.

This kiss nowhere near matched the one of quiet hunger he'd given her in the car. His mouth was hard, his lips hot, tongue seeking, taking, punishing. Justin pushed her from the wall and a few steps across the room, until the backs of her knees connected with the sofa.

Justin smiled a wide smile as he pushed her down to the couch, at the same time unfastening her coverall. The coverall came down, and then the silk under-leggings she wore beneath it. Justin wriggled coverall and leggings around until they were off, and all Deanna wore was her sleeveless tunic.

Justin looped her knees over his arms, laid her back on the rather lumpy cushions, and knelt between her legs. He kissed the insides of her thighs with the same strong kisses before he lowered his head and fastened his mouth over her opening.

Deanna let out a strangled gasp. She'd never felt *anything* like this before. His mouth was scalding, the friction of his tongue grating, his teeth scraping her tightening clit.

She rocked her hips, as he had done, wanting to drive herself up and into his beautiful mouth.

"*Justin!*"

She couldn't take it. Deanna squirmed and wriggled, but she couldn't get away from his mouth, his tongue. And she didn't want to.

Justin wasn't going anywhere. He licked and tasted her, drinking her spice, loving how wet she was for him. Her come flowed into his mouth, his lady opening up to a man for the first time. Justin knew it was her first time, her reaction telling him that she'd never felt the amazing wildness of orgasm.

Her cries turned incoherent, and Justin smiled to himself as he suckled her swollen clit. The clit was pink and delectable, her pussy framed by soft but wiry dark hair. Some women shaved for their Shareem, but Justin liked the tickling feeling of Deanna's hair as he drank.

He licked his way around either side of her opening and then fastened his mouth to the wet folds and drank some more.

Her echoing cries turned to whimpering moans, an inexperienced woman quickly finding her first explosion of passion.

Justin could have feasted on her all night, but he eased back, licked her clean, and raised his head.

"Aw damn," he said, feeling himself grin as wide as his mouth could go. "Now I need another shower."

* * * * *

Showering with Deanna was good. Justin towed her inside in her silk undertunic, the rest of her clothes a pile on his sofa.

The wet tunic came off, and she stood with him, naked, while water poured over her tight little body. She was a patroller, so she was strong, but her honed muscles made her slim and pretty, and the breasts that tightened in the water were full and round.

So good to wash soap over her body, good to have her soap him in return. His shower wasn't that big, but they managed, sliding against each other when they needed to move, laughing at the tight space. No complaint from Justin.

He wanted to finish this, wanted to take her in a deep, satisfying fucking. But not yet.

Justin wanted to learn her, to let her learn him. He wanted to teach her about pleasure, but he also wanted her to have fun.

He thought of ways to play—maybe tie her hands then squirt her with whipped cream and honey and lick her clean. He might blindfold her, maybe, and then spank her and show her how much fun it was.

Right now they were playing at soaping each other down. Again, no complaints.

The slick soap let Justin glide his hands up and down her wet body, find the warmth beneath her bosom. He lifted the weight of her breasts and splayed his hands over them, closing fingers around her nipples.

She roved her touch over him in return, sliding over his backside, which she found fascinating, and around to his cock again. He'd teach her how to spank him too.

Justin pressed her back against the smooth wall and kissed her. He liked that she was already learning to kiss him back, opening her lips without hesitation.

"Justin, I need to talk to you."

Deanna's voice was a whisper, she breathless from the kisses.

Not now.

She didn't seem inclined to keep trying to talk. Justin kissed her again, hands sliding down her body to the join of her legs.

"We need to make sure you're clean," he said, and she smiled.

Regular soap could sting her sensitive pussy, especially when he'd made it swell, but Justin had special soap that would clean without hurt. He squirted it on his hand and put his hand between her legs.

She widened her stance, and Justin leaned into her against the shower wall while he washed her. And damned if his fingers didn't happen to slip inside her, to find the tight walls, to make her drag in a breath.

He played there, two fingers only—Deanna was tight. He had some toys that would loosen her a bit and make her more pliant for harder play. But not right now. Now was for stroking, teasing, and teaching.

Justin kissed her, the water trickling down his face, as he rubbed his thumb over her clit.

When she came, his mouth was on hers, and he caught her cries on his tongue. She squirmed against him too, the stiff pole of his cock sandwiched between them.

The little sweetie wrapped both hands around it and started to stroke. She learned fast. Before the last of her cries had died, Justin rested his forehead against the tile wall and came and came.

They wound down together, letting the shower wash them clean, until Justin finally snapped off the water.

Justin rubbed Deanna dry with the fluffy towel hanging outside the shower, not minding that there was only the one. He didn't mind being damp while he wrapped Deanna in the towel's folds and kissed her warm lips.

"I did really come over to talk to you," Deanna said when her mouth was free. Her voice was a throaty murmur.

"Let's talk later." Justin said, rubbing a drop from the bridge of her nose. "I'm not in the mood to be serious."

Deanna watched him for a moment longer, eyes soft. "About Lillian," she said.

Chapter Nine

The words connected with Justin's brain after a few more rubs. He stopped, the towel pressed against her breasts.

If she'd wanted to kill the mood, Deanna couldn't have a done a better job. The heat in his body started to fade, his cock — finally — to deflate.

"What?" he asked in a careful voice.

"I know why you came back to Bor Narga," Deanna said.

Justin grabbed her, towel and all, and propelled her out of the bathroom and into his tiny bedroom. He half-lifted, half-tossed her onto the bed then climbed over her, the towel the only thing between his dripping body and hers.

"Tell me," he said.

"Lillian was K-48," Deanna said, looking up at him without fear. "I read your files, and hers. You fell in love with each other and started a relationship. But that was against the rules, so they transferred her out of your section. Am I right?"

"Yes."

Justin remembered the bleak day the researchers had told him that Lillian had been moved beyond his reach. He'd had to badger them before they'd even give him that much information.

They'd taken away the only thing that had put any warmth into Justin's existence—seeing Lillian, whom he'd refused to call K-48. The admins at DNAmo had ripped her from him, leaving him alone and bereft, and they hadn't cared.

Justin hadn't been able to do a damn thing about it. He'd raged at them until they'd subdued him with shocks and drugs, then he'd had to sit there, alone, and grieve. She'd told him about her pregnancy before she'd gone, so he'd worried about that as well.

"You came back to Bor Narga to find her," Deanna said.

"Maybe." The relief that Deanna hadn't mentioned Sybellie relaxed him a little, but Justin knew he needed to remain cautious. "Does it matter? It was years ago. DNAmo is closed, all that shit over. Now Lillian is just someone I knew. I got to wondering what happened to her."

"So you left a decent life on Sirius to be restricted again on Bor Narga to find her?"

Justin made himself shrug, though he knew she could feel his pounding heart. "Sure. My lover, Shela, died. I was lonely. I thought maybe I could hook up with Lillian again."

Deanna watched him with dark eyes that were full of . . . hurt? "You're telling me that you traveled five light years back to a planet where you're the equivalent of a prisoner on parole to find a woman you haven't seen in twenty-some years? Because you wanted to 'hook up?'"

"Yes," Justin said.

"You are so full of bullshit."

Deanna struggled to get up, but Justin caught her wrists and held her down.

"Maybe I found something better," he said. "Like a pretty patroller who can't keep her cute nose out of my business."

The hurt in her eyes returned, shoving aside the anger. "Like I said, Justin, you are full of bullshit."

"It's not bullshit that I like you. That's why I wanted you to come tonight. That's why I dream about you with your stun gun full of whipped cream."

He nuzzled her, trying to let his voice go seductive. He was Shareem. He could charm her out of her anger, make her forget all about Lillian, make her stop wanting to dig deeper into his past.

But Deanna was damn stubborn. "Why didn't you tell me?"

"Oh, right, tell a patroller I'd come back to hunt down a woman taken away from me at DNAmo because we got too close? I didn't want Lillian to get any shit thrown at her because of me." Justin tightened his grip on Deanna's wrists. "I still don't."

"That's not what I meant. I meant, why didn't you tell *me*? Maybe I wouldn't have ridden you so hard."

Justin growled and tried to smile. "Don't make my mind go *there*. I'm barely holding it in."

"What I'm trying to explain, Justin, is that if you really want to find this woman, I can help you."

"Help me? Help me how?"

"I have resources, access to databases, clearances that you never will. If you want to find Lillian, *I* can find her."

She was serious. "Why would you do that?" he asked.

"Because I read your DNAmo files. I don't think it was fair to either of you that they split you up. And because maybe if you find her, you'll go off and live with her somewhere, and stop screwing up my life." Deanna was breathing hard, her body rigid under his, but her eyes were shining with tears.

"Hey." Justin let his voice grow gentle. "I know I got you into trouble. I'm sorry." He should add, *You go home and work on keeping your job, and I promise I'll leave you alone.*

The words wouldn't come out. Justin gripped her wrists, not wanting to let go. Having her walk out, and not come back . . . He didn't even want to think about it. Patroller or not, Justin liked Deanna. Wanted her. Wanted her *here*.

"I can't lie to you," Deanna said, so softly that Justin had to lean to her. "I know why you really want to find Lillian."

No, she couldn't. Justin hated that she thought he wanted to find Lillian because he was still in love with her, but the real reason was too dangerous for her to know. "I told you," he said. "I was lonely. I wanted to find out what happened to her."

"And you want to talk to her about your child."

Justin had her off the bed and hauled against the wall before he knew what he was doing. Terror beat through him so hard he couldn't see.

"What the *fuck*?"

Deanna lifted her chin. "I figured out that Lillian had a baby, about nine months after she left DNAmo. I know that Lillian only ever did the sex experiments with you. I know that the baby would be about twenty-four by now, and I know that you went to the Vistara to watch a group of young women. Which one was yours?"

Justin found his hand around her slender throat. "Don't you touch her. Don't you go near her. *Do you understand me?*"

Deanna didn't look away. "I wouldn't. I wouldn't, Justin. I know you'd be terminated if anyone found out."

"I don't give a damn about me. *She'd* be killed. She'd be dissected, and studied, and not allowed to live . . ."

His breath gave out, as though he'd just sprinted a mile straight uphill.

"I know," Deanna said. He still had his hand at her throat, but her voice was clear. "It's not her fault."

"That her father is a fucking Shareem?"

"Not her fault that the laws are all screwed up."

"What are you saying, Patroller? That I can trust you? That her life is safe with you?"

"Yes," Deanna whispered. "That's exactly what I'm saying."

Justin stared at her, his lungs burning. She looked right back at him, no fear in her eyes. Worry, yes; fear, no. And truth. Deanna wanted to help him, just as she'd offered to when he'd been in her detention cell.

Help me help you, she'd said.

But that had been nothing to do with Sybellie. He had to protect his daughter, at all costs.

"You leave her the hell alone. You leave Lillian the hell alone. You've never heard of her, all right?" He leaned closer to Deanna, her scent driving him crazy, but his fear making him even more crazy. "Stay the fuck out of my life."

More tears filled her eyes, but Deanna didn't break down, not this tough patroller. "You asked me to come here tonight."

"I made a mistake." Justin wanted to let her go, to back away, but he couldn't, not yet.

"Why did you ask me?" She blinked back the tears. "If you're looking for Lillian, if you're trying to keep me from figuring out what you're doing, why did you ask me?"

Because he'd wanted her. Deanna intrigued him, called to him. Kissing her in his living room then touching her in the car had aroused Justin's deepest needs, not just for a woman, but for *her*.

Maybe the danger of being with Deanna, because she was a patroller, excited him. Or maybe he wanted to dominate her to get her back for dominating him.

He knew that neither of those explanations was true, even as he tried to make himself believe them. What he'd had with Shela had been wonderful, and Justin could feel something like that building between himself and Deanna. But he couldn't risk it.

Deanna's body trembled under his hands. Her hair was down, wet, snaking around her body. When she'd worn the veil, she'd looked sweet and feminine, her eyes soft.

Right now she was sexy as sin, beautiful innocence experiencing her first touch of a man. Justin wanted to reach for that sensuality and bring it out of her, show her how to revel in it, to show her how to find the deepest pleasure imaginable.

He wanted to teach her, to unwrap her layer by layer, until she was totally open to him.

He wanted Deanna.

Justin made himself let her go. He stepped back, his gut clenching, his body shaking.

"Go," he said.

She stared at him. She was naked, damp from the shower, delectable.

"*Go,*" he said, the word jerking out of him.

Deanna stood there, frozen against the wall, damn beautiful and looking at him like he was crazy.

Which he was. Justin turned away, grabbed a tunic, pulled it over his naked body, and slammed out of the room. He barreled out of the whole apartment to the hot street, in the dark, where he started walking, who the hell cared where.

* * * * *

Justin ended up at Eland and Jeanne's. Jeanne had a nice little apartment in one of the better streets in Pas City, which had sun awnings and storm shielding. Jeanne never had to sweep out her front room after every sandstorm, as Justin did. Blowing sand had learned how to find every crack around Justin's door and burst in, uninvited.

Justin pushed the buzzer and heard Eland's big voice through the com. "Enter."

The door rolled back, and Justin walked through a vestibule to a door on the far end. The front door closed and the rear door opened at the same time, ushering Justin into the living room.

Eland and Jeanne were having sex in it.

The big Eland sat on a straight-backed chair, with Jeanne straddling him. They moved rapidly, Jeanne working Eland deep into her.

Her head moved on her slender neck, her naked breasts with dusky nipples pressing Eland's chest. The heavy ring in her left nipple both pulled on her breast and ground into Eland, who didn't seem to mind.

Eland didn't look around at Justin's entrance. Eland's gaze was all for Jeanne, his Shareem eyes fixed on her with deep love.

A normal human would have averted his gaze, expressed surprise or disgust, or taken himself out of the apartment.

But Justin was Shareem, and the pheromones pouring from Eland and Jeanne, thick and harsh, kept him in place. Plus, he was keyed up from his encounter with Deanna and Deanna's revelations, plus he'd still not had full sex, and Deanna had left him burning.

"You could have warned me," Justin growled. He jerked the tunic from his body before he even realized he had. His cock stood out ramrod straight, and Justin closed his hand around it.

Doing that made him remember how Deanna had touched him and brought him to peak in his living room. Which made him remember the fun in the shower, which brought him full circle to the anguish and fear of her announcement that she knew about Sybellie.

Then his brain took him back to how much fun it would be for Deanna to be here sucking him off— and he her—while they watched Eland and Jeanne enjoying the hell out of each other in their living room.

"That's it, baby," Eland said, still watching Jeanne. "Take me deep."

Jeanne was far gone in passion. Shareem were big, and Eland's huge cock was buried pretty hard inside her. Jeanne's skin shone with perspiration, as did Eland's.

Jeanne moved her hands on Eland's neck, and Justin saw that cuffs enclosed her wrists with a chain between them. Real cuffs, not the playful, fuzzy ones Justin used. Eland was level three, which meant the rough stuff.

Justin moved to the table beyond them, caught up lube they'd left there, and squirted it onto his hand. Watching was nowhere near as much fun as doing, but Justin leaned his ass on the table and tried to let the tingling pleasure of his hand on himself calm his fear. He needed to be calm to figure out what to do about Deanna.

"I think he likes it, baby," Eland rumbled.

Jeanne, eyes closed, submersed in deepest pleasure, didn't answer. It was an even bet she didn't even realize Justin was there.

Eland rose on strong legs and wrapped Jeanne's legs around him. Her eyes opened wide as he pressed deeper still.

"Justin," Eland said breathlessly. "Plug."

A plug waited on the table, a small, flexible one. Justin caught it up, using the lube to wet it.

Justin was ready to hand it to Eland so he could do the honors, but Eland put his hands around Jeanne's ass and spread her a little. Eland's lubed finger went between her buttocks, rubbing to soften and open her.

"Put it in," Eland said.

He was far gone too. Justin placed the plug between two fingers, steadied his hand on Jeanne's ass where Eland opened her, and slid the little thing into place.

Jeanne squealed her pleasure and wriggled on Eland. A smile spread across Eland's face. "Aw, yeah, that's good. Thank you."

Justin backed off and let them have their fun, but he stayed within range of their warmth and let their pheromones and his bathe him in mindless physical pleasure. He closed his eyes, envisioning Deanna, on her knees, her mouth around his cock.

Aw, fuck. Justin's seed shot out of him and onto the floor, just as Eland and Jeanne hit their peaks together and hung on to each other hard.

Justin let out a long breath, eyes still closed. He whispered, "Deanna," and let his mind go blank for a few minutes.

When he could think again, Justin unwound his sore fingers as Eland resumed the chair, Eland and Jeanne kissing and cooing.

"Sorry," Justin said.

Jeanne turned her head, her hands still in the cuffs, her eyes heavy with afterglow. "For what?"

"Your floor."

She laughed, which shook her body, and Eland gave Justin a beatific smile. "That's what the towels are for," she said.

Justin looked down. Practical Jeanne had spread towels all around the chair, knowing that sex was messy. Wise woman.

"I'll just borrow your shower," Justin said, heading for the back.

The other two didn't answer. They were cuddling and kissing, enjoying the moment. Justin didn't mind watching sex, but what they were doing now was private, emotional. Loving.

What he wanted to explore with Deanna.

Justin soaped off in their shower, dried himself with the hot air dryers in the walls, and pulled on his tunic again. By the time he reentered the living room, the chair and towels were gone, and the lovers were lounging on the sofa.

Eland had at least covered his cock with a loose pair of leggings, but Jeanne sat, naked and demure, against the pillows. She'd learned long ago not to be inhibited around Shareem. She had shining dark hair, mussed now from lovemaking, but none between her legs. Eland liked a bare pussy.

Jeanne looked up at Justin, her dark eyes filled with contentment. "You changed your mind about the threesome, then?"

"I came to find out if you'd spoken to your friend, the one who might have known Lillian."

"Too bad—about the threesome I mean. Yes, I did talk to her. She agreed to meet you. I was going to call you and then . . ."

Eland was watching Justin with a measuring look. "You sure you want to find Lillian? DNAmo was a long time ago, and a lot has changed."

"I'm not looking for her to continue what we once had," Justin said, knowing the truth of it. "If we had anything more than mutual loneliness in the first place. I want to talk to her, make sure she's okay . . ."

He closed his mouth under Eland's scrutiny. No one knew about Sybellie but Braden and Elisa—and now Deanna. Justin had told the other Shareem that he'd returned to Bor Narga to hunt up Lillian, nothing more. They all thought him insane but accepted his explanation.

Jeanne stood up, leaned down to kiss Eland, and gave Justin a wink. "We'll meet my friend at Judith's. Which means I have to wear clothes. *Judith* doesn't mind me without, but people on the subway just don't understand."

She laughed as Eland flicked her nipple ring with one finger, then she sauntered out of the room to get ready.

"Seriously, Justin," Eland said, once she'd gone. "I'm all for you finding Lillian, but be careful. The less the patrollers watch us right now, the better."

Justin knew what he meant. Rees, the Shareem who was more or less their leader, was a Shareem of no level—another DNAmo experiment gone awry.

Recently, Rees had began working to get the Shareem off planet, to someplace they could live without so many restrictions. Not an easy task, and if any of them were caught, all Shareem could be terminated. Justin, who knew people on Sirius who could help the Shareem, had agreed to assist.

But Justin couldn't leave the planet right now. Not until he figured out what to do about Sybellie.

And now Deanna knew about her.

Jeanne returned, wearing a silk sheath that hugged her body but covered her to Bor Nargan standards. Eland donned a tunic, lent Justin some leggings, and they all left together.

Chapter Ten

Judith's place was full tonight, with both Shareem and the dock workers, male and female, who liked to hang out there. Shareem attracted women, the male workers weren't ashamed to pick up Shareem leavings, and the female workers sized up both Shareem and the human males.

Judith gestured to a table in a shadowy corner where a Bor Nargan woman waited alone. Jeanne waved at the woman and led them there.

When Judith brought ale to the four of them, she paused to duck toward Jeanne and kiss her full on the lips. "After?" Judith asked.

Jeanne nodded without worry and sipped her ale.

"Wait a minute," Justin asked before Judith could walk away. "What happened to 'Mitch doesn't like it?'"

"Oh, he doesn't mind Jeanne," Judith said. "He just doesn't want a Shareem's testosterone-laden hands all over me. Mitch likes Jeanne, and likes to watch us go."

Eland grinned at Justin. "It's a great show."

"I'll bet."

Once upon a time, Justin might have begged a front-row seat, but now that his life was complicated, Justin drank his ale and waited impatiently for the conversation to turn to what he'd come here for.

Jeanne's friend must have become used to Shareem—and Jeanne—because she didn't look shocked in the slightest at either the kiss or the obvious appointment for a threesome later. Jeanne introduced the woman as Mira, a freelance sailor on transport ships.

Mira's face was lined with experience, age, and travel, but she had lively dark eyes, and her hair held no gray. Her job explained her unworried expression. She'd have been to many planets and seen practices far beyond what Bor Narga's inhibited stance on sex allowed.

"I think the woman I knew used to work for DNAmo," Mira said once introductions were done. "She lived on Madallin Row with her mom and dad."

Justin's heart beat faster. "That's her. Do you have any idea where she is now?"

"Sorry. Wish I did. She was a good friend."

He tried to hide his acute disappointment. "When did you last see her?"

"About fifteen years ago," Mira said. "I shipped out with a company that did runs in the Paladias system, and was there for a year or so. When I got back, Lillian's mom had died—her dad had gone a few months before that, I heard from her neighbors—and Lillian had moved out. No one in the neighborhood knew where she'd gone. Someone said the mountains, but when I had the chance to go out there, a couple years later, I never saw her. I looked, but didn't find her." Mira shrugged. "She might have gone off-world. I didn't try too hard, because my life had moved on, and I figured hers had too. But do you want me to ask around?"

Justin turned his ale glass on the table. "I don't want her getting into trouble because a Shareem is asking for her."

Mira sent him a little smile. "I can be discreet."

"Be *really* discreet."

"You can trust her," Jeanne said. "She understands."

"I do," Mira said. "So, Justin, you busy for the rest of the night? You for hire?"

She made him sound like a taxi. Justin had urged Deanna to engage him for his services, but when Mira asked for it, the appeal did a complete turnaround.

"Sorry," Justin said. "Not tonight."

"He's not been interested in sex very much at all lately," Jeanne said. "Poor guy. He must not be feeling well."

"Yeah, that's it," Justin said. "I'm getting over something."

"You two leave him alone," Eland rumbled. "Drink up. It's on me. If you want a Shareem, I'm handy. But only with Jeanne too."

Mira laughed. "No thanks. You're cute, Jeanne, but I don't lean that way. Maybe later, Shareem." She winked at Justin then absorbed herself in finishing off her ale and signaling for more. The woman was a serious drinker.

Justin finished his ale more slowly, noting that Mira was on about her seventh by the time he quit the place and went back to his apartment to think about what she'd said.

The mountains. Not extremely specific, but it was a place to start.

Deanna wasn't in the apartment when Justin reached it. He shucked his clothes and lay down on the bed, her fresh scent still lingering on the sheets where he'd pressed her. He closed his eyes, and sighed when his cock began to rise again.

* * * * *

Deanna had spent some time after Justin left his apartment searching it. She didn't know why she wanted to, but the ache in her heart made her need to do *something*.

She didn't find much. Justin's apartment was bare of anything but necessities, and he had little in the way of clothes or personal belongings.

Behind his bed, she found a wall compartment that slid open to her touch. When closed, the compartment blended seamlessly into the wall, but the catch to open it wasn't hidden. Inside the compartment, she found two boxes.

One was about two feet on a side and made of wood, an incongruity on Bor Narga. The box was not locked, and Deanna opened its lid to find an interior lined with black cloth and divided into sections, a top tray lifting out to reveal a deeper space beneath.

The things that lay in the slots in these sections made her still. He had handcuffs, several pairs. Not the functional kind that Deanna carried to subdue arrestees, but thick cuffs lined with velvet, cloth, or fake fur. Each had a slim chain between the cuffs that looked almost like jewelry.

Straps, both leather and cloth, were folded into another slot. In another she found a small, velvet-lined box that contained three small spheres. What those were for, she had no idea.

She also found the wands—small, slender ones as well as shorter, wider plugs. She stared at them a moment, before realizing they were for insertion . . . into various places.

Deanna's imagination conjured Justin's fingers warm on her while he carefully slid one of the wands inside her.

She shivered and opened her eyes, which had drifted closed for some reason.

Another slot carried tubes of lubrication, and another held three small glass bottles. She worked out the stopper on one bottle, smiling in delight when she breathed in the heady aroma of cardamom and other spices.

Justin smoothed these oils on the lady he pleasured, she presumed. He'd restrain her with the cuffs and use the plugs to fill her, while he worked the oil into her skin. The straps? For teasing and tickling, or for something harsher?

Deanna pictured herself lying facedown on his bed, her wrists fixed to headboard by the soft cuffs, while he drew the straps down her bare back. She'd be filled with the plug, warm from his caresses, waiting for his kisses on her skin, and for him to fill her himself . . .

Deanna shuddered, nearly dropping the bottle of oil. She quickly put in the stopper and returned everything to the box where she'd found it.

The second box in the wall compartment was smaller and made of plastic. This too was not locked. Deanna opened it and found . . . Justin.

Printed photographs, which they still used on Sirius and other backwoods planets, lay scattered on top of souvenirs. The first photograph showed Justin, grinning, wearing a body-concealing work coverall, looking so *normal*.

More shots of Justin—in a bar, holding up a glass of ale, surrounded by other laughing men; with his arm around a brown-haired woman who wore the same kind of coverall; of the same woman in a short tunic at an ocean, then one of Justin, wearing short leggings and nothing else. He balanced on a rock, laughing, while the ocean crashed behind him.

The woman must be Shela, the woman he'd lived with for fifteen years. They both looked so happy.

The other things in the box were bits and pieces of Justin's life on Sirius — plastic entrance discs for various shows, his work ID for his job on the space docks then the permit to start his own offloading company, plus the deed to a house a little outside the city.

Deanna looked closer at the deed — Justin still owned the house. That was a blatant violation of laws on Bor Narga, but not on Sirius. Touchy if the issue ever came to a trial.

At the bottom of the box was a faded piece of silk — a Bor Nargan veil, Deanna realized when she pulled it out. The veil was old but had been kept with care. With it was a small plastic card, a note of some kind maybe, though Deanna could see nothing on it when she held it up to the light. She'd need a computer to read it.

The veil and card gave her an idea. She folded the silk around the card and tucked both into the pocket inside her coverall. The veil was so fine it folded to nothing.

Deanna closed the box and slid it back into its place, shutting the wall compartment again, before she left Justin's apartment for the darkness of the desert night.

Pas City had cooled from the terrible heat of the day, the district and markets coming alive with people, color, lights. But Deanna turned her back on

the laughter pouring down the streets and headed
home.

She entered her apartment quietly to find Reda
in the living room watching a vid.

"Sleeping," Reda said, answering Deanna's
unasked question. Deanna nodded. She looked in on
her mother, saw Kayla indeed sleeping heavily, and
went on to her bedroom.

Deanna brought up her computer, unfolded the
veil from her pocket, stuck the silk into the full
scanner, and read the secrets it revealed.

Chapter Eleven

Not surprisingly, the DNA on the veil matched the DNA for Lillian Passan. Perhaps she'd left the veil behind at DNAmo one day, and Justin had kept it for her, or perhaps she'd given it to Justin as a remembrance gift.

Deanna set the veil aside and keyed in her authorization code to search the highly restricted DNA databases for all of Bor Narga. Very few had the clearance, but Deanna had qualified for it—something else she might lose if her captain decided to fire her.

The DNA database found a partial match for Lillian's DNA in a young woman called Sybellie, who had the same birth date as the anonymous birth recorded at the backstreet medic's. The girl's mother was listed as anonymous, father unknown, and the database showed she'd been adopted as an infant by a Vistara family.

Why a Vistara family would adopt a working-class illegitimate child, Deanna didn't know, but perhaps they were kindhearted, or couldn't have children themselves, or . . . Who knew?

The holopic of Sybellie showed her to be one of the young women Deanna had seen at the coffeehouse. Sybellie had seemed to be accepted by her friends and happy—Deanna could find no evidence in her records that she'd had difficulties in school or was thought inferior.

There was no information listed for Sybellie's biological father—no name, no DNA record. That was not unusual in the matriarchal society of Bor Narga, where the mother was the most important connection. Money, land, inheritance, and names came through the woman.

The father would be listed only if he came from a good family connection or had a lot of money for his children to inherit. If the mother did not want the father to have responsibility for or even access to the child, she could leave him out of the records altogether. Many births among working-class women had no father listed.

No one, it seemed, had bothered to check Sybellie's DNA for a father match. No one had cared. Lillian was the important person in the equation, not the man who'd gotten her pregnant. Though, in this case, no one had much cared who the anonymous mother was either.

Deanna did not run the search for the father now. She did not want to risk leaving any trace of her search, and lead those who policed the databases back to Justin.

Although, they might not notice. Deanna's opinion of the people who watched the government databases for illegal activity wasn't high. When Deanna worked with them to track down criminals, they took a lot of things for granted and didn't look beyond their assumptions.

Even so, she didn't chance it.

Deanna went back to Lillian's DNA record and ran the search for her DNA again.

After about two hours of scrolling, backtracking, and tracing through linked databases, her back aching, she found another match.

* * * * *

Justin ignored the buzzing of his com that woke him out of half-drunk slumber the next morning. The caller was Deanna—she didn't bother to disguise her number.

He ached to see her again, but some part of him feared to. He was falling for the woman, *needed* her, but she knew too much, and any danger to Sybellie made him wild.

Then again, if he kept Deanna in his sights, kept her sated with pleasure, he could control her and what she knew. Maybe.

Either recourse was dangerous.

Justin reached for the com to answer it just as it went silent. His thumb hovered over the button to return the call then he sighed and lowered his hand back to his side.

Damn it.

Time to start moving. Justin dragged himself out of bed, put himself through the shower, dressed, and decided to hit the street to find breakfast at a vendor's cart.

His door opened before he could reach for the control, to reveal Deanna standing in the sunshine holding two coffees. She held one out to him.

"Ready?" she asked.

Justin braced himself on the doorframe and blinked down at her, the half-hangover pounding through his head. "Ready for what? Are you arresting me? Luring me into your paddy wagon with coffee?"

"What are you mumbling about? I hired a car. You want to go up to the Vistara, don't you? It's almost time."

Sure enough, a tiny hovercar waited a few feet down from Justin's apartment door. "What the fuck?"

Deanna thrust the coffee into his hand. "If you want to go to the Vistara, better to let me drive you in a private car than get caught walking around up there. You were going to try to go again today, weren't you?"

Yes. "I was giving it some thought."

"Then get in the car."

Justin took a gulp of coffee. He grimaced, the brew cheap, even for Bor Nargan coffee, but it cut through the haze in his head.

Deanna walked off toward the car, giving him a nice view of her ass in the tight coveralls. He walked after her, trying not to stumble, and the passenger door of the car slid open for him. Saying nothing, Justin climbed inside.

This wasn't a patrol car. It was a private conveyance, meant for a driver and a couple of passengers, nothing luxurious about it.

Justin drank his coffee in silence, though his pulse raced and his mind jumped from worried thought to worried thought.

If he didn't talk, didn't even say the word *Vistara*, Deanna couldn't tell anyone, without lying, that he wanted to go to an area restricted to him. If she, a patroller, drove him up there, Justin couldn't do anything about it, could he? Not his fault that a patroller dragged him through the district for reasons of her own.

Deanna slid into the driver's seat, sealed the doors, and touched the controls. The hovercar rose, rather bumpily, and slid slowly through the crowded streets to the main thoroughfare.

Justin watched Deanna's slim fingers tap controls as she programmed her destination. When she sat back to let the car take over, she reached into her coverall and pulled something out of her pocket.

"I'm guessing you'll want that back," Deanna said, laying Lillian's scarf and her coded note about Sybellie in his lap.

"Shit." Justin snatched up both, the silk of the veil soft on his fingers. "Where the hell did you get these?"

"From the compartment in your bedroom, behind your bed."

"You searched my apartment?"

"You made me angry," Deanna said. "So I did a search. I don't know why, but it made me feel better. I found those. I couldn't read the card, no matter how I tried to break the code, but the scarf was Lillian's."

"I know." He stuffed card and veil inside his tunic pocket.

"It gave me an idea of how to trace her."

Now fear joined the roiling inside him. "I told you, I don't want you tracing her."

"And I told you, I'm not going to tell anyone about Sybellie. It wouldn't be fair to her." She adjusted a control to move around another, slower, car. "I know why you're worried, and you're absolutely right."

Justin opened his mouth then closed it again without speaking. He wanted to trust her, but he didn't trust himself. He was forming affection for Deanna, the hot little patroller, who had so far proved that she didn't mindlessly follow the rules.

And she was hot. Wait, did he think that already? Maybe he was letting his need for sex with her override his common sense.

Who was he kidding? Need for sex with her was absolutely messing with his common sense. Being in the close space with her, breathing her scent . . . His hangover was dissolving under a rush of need.

"What else did you find while you were searching my place?" he asked.

Her little, shy, sideways glance made his blood heat. "One or two things, in that wooden box. I didn't understand what they were all for."

Aw, she was so cute when she blushed. Deanna had lost her businesslike stance, and had once again become the woman who'd asked him to show her how to bring him off. "Make an appointment with me, sweetheart, and I'll teach you all about the things in my magic box."

Deanna's blush deepened, and a for a moment, he thought she'd agree. But then she lost her smile and looked serious. "I wanted to ask you about your lifemate, Shela. She never had a child, did she? But obviously you can make one, and you wouldn't have had the sterility inoculations on Sirius."

The delightful thoughts of watching Deanna sift through his box of accoutrements while he showed her what each plug, strap, ring, and clamp was for, fled.

"No," he said in a quiet voice. "Shela couldn't. That was . . . hard on her."

"I'm sorry." Deanna sounded like she meant it. "You stayed with her, though. I mean, you knew you could have kids, but not with her."

"Yes, I stayed." He wondered what was going on behind those pretty eyes. "Not her fault, and I wanted to be with her. Why are you asking?"

"No reason." She swerved the car up the last of the hill to the double street where the coffeehouse lay. "We're here."

Deanna pulled the car over, parking it behind hovercars in which Vistara women were driven half a block by their chauffeurs to go shopping. The coffeehouse was open and full, and the four young women sat at their table by the window.

Justin sat back in his seat and slowly let out his breath. Deanna had parked closer to the coffeehouse than he usually got to stand. The car's tinted windows hid them from the passersby on the street, but unlike Brianne's car, its windows didn't have so much shielding that they blocked out the windows of the coffeehouse.

Justin saw Sybellie clearly. She laughed at something one of her friends said, her mouth open as she clenched her hands around her coffee cup.

She was so beautiful. Justin saw much of Lillian in her, but her eyes were the same shape as the ones that looked back at him from the mirror in his bathroom. The rose color she chose for her veils suited her, matching her pink lips and . . .

"She paints her fingernails," Justin said in tender wonder. "Pink to match her veil."

"I see that."

He felt himself grinning like an idiot. "Am I supposed to say, *that looks nice, honey,* or tell her she shouldn't spend all her time on manicures? Damn it, I don't know how to be a father."

"I don't know what you're supposed to say. I don't have kids either."

The sadness in Deanna's voice tugged at him. "What did your mom say to you?" he asked.

Deanna glanced at her fingernails, which were smooth but short. "I've never had my nails done, so nothing about that. She did once tell me, *that's a nice pistol, honey, but don't spend all your time at the firing range.*"

Justin had to laugh, even though her voice had gone sadder still. He rested his hand on Deanna's thigh, liking the wiry strength of it, remembering her in the shower, her skin soft and feminine.

She was giving him a gift, he realized, letting him see Sybellie without interference. He was going to kiss her for that. And more.

Sybellie was telling her friends something, her eyes animated, hands moving as she related whatever was the funny story. He wanted to hear it, wanted to see her roll her eyes and say, *Dad!* when he asked her about it.

He wanted it so much it was killing him.

"It's a hell of a thing," he said softly. "I want to see her, talk to her, hug her—just *be* with her. But I also want to protect her. And I can only do that by staying away from her."

He felt Deanna's gaze on him. She was looking at him in understanding, sympathy even. No, she was definitely not like any other patroller he'd ever met.

The girls were leaving. The four of them walked out, pausing outside the coffeehouse to talk still more.

Justin couldn't take his eyes off Sybellie. She was so young, so innocent and pretty. Lillian had been much the same, but Lillian had already been hardened when she was twenty, having to grub for a living. Sybellie was soft, unused to the world, untouched. Free. Happy.

There was much hugging, and then two of the girls walked away, their arms linked. Sybellie and her other friend remained, still talking. At times, they both were talking at the same time without realizing it, and Justin laughed.

He watched her, his heart full, his daughter three steps away from him, and she never knew it.

Sybellie's friend walked away, Sybellie waving. She scanned the street, as though deciding which direction to go. Her gaze swept over the car, not seeing Justin behind the tinted glass, not knowing he sat there, his entire being aching for her.

Deanna's fingers closed around his and squeezed. Justin clung to her hand, glad she was with him, knowing she'd done this for him.

A man walked past the car, an off-worlder by his clothes. He stopped and looked at Sybellie. Justin noticed him only because the man took a few quick steps forward, put himself in front of Sybellie, and started talking to her.

A growl rose in his throat. Maybe the guy knew her, friend of her parents, or something.

But Sybellie was drawing back, giving him a look of distaste, and then disgust, then fear. She tried to turn away, but the man grabbed her arm.

Justin was halfway out of the car when Deanna's full weight landed on him. "Justin, don't you dare!"

Justin fought to untangle himself. "He needs to get the hell away from her."

"I know. But let me. *Let me.*"

"Damn it, Deanna—"

Deanna let him go but locked the passenger door at the same time she opened her own. "You stay there. This is my job."

Justin knew she was right. If he leapt out and accosted the man, he would be arrested, and Sybellie might be exposed. But he couldn't just sit here . . .

Deanna was around the car, her stun gun held casually in her hand, her patroller's swagger in place. Justin held his breath, but at the same time he felt a surge of pride as Deanna moved to the man and got right in his face.

That's my girl . . .

* * * * *

The off-worlder was the kind Deanna didn't like—arrogant, superior-acting, so sure that Bor Narga, in spite of its advanced culture, was backward because it was ruled by women. Well, he was going to learn a thing or two.

Deanna stepped to him and used a practiced grip on his wrist to make him open his hand. The man winced, and his eyes widened in sudden pain, but he let go of Sybellie.

"What the fuck?" He had an accent, but he spoke Bor Nargan very clearly. It sounded like he'd practiced the swear words.

"Bor Nargan women aren't to be touched without permission," Deanna said in her crisp, Patroller First Class voice. "That's on page two of your *Traveler's Guide to Bor Narga*, which was handed out to you on your transport. You read it, right?"

"Hey, bitch, you shouldn't touch *me*."

He was red with anger, and Sybellie started to edge away.

"It's all right," Deanna told her. "He's just a dickhead. Don't disrupt your day because of him."

"You should be polite to me, sweetheart," the man said, "or you won't get anyone else coming to this backwoods planet."

"On page thirty-six, it says you can be arrested for being an asshole," Deanna said. "Now clear off the Vistara before you tempt me."

He tapped a badge on his tunic. "Fuck you. *This* means I get to go anywhere I want to on this rock."

"*That* is a Class Three pass. Meaning you can go anywhere you want as long as you follow Bor Nargan law, which includes obeying any directive given to you by a patroller. If you disobey my directive, I get to stun you, arrest you, take you to detention, and then throw your butt *off* this rock."

"What are you going to do, sweetie, put me in cuffs? Maybe I'd like that."

Why when Justin teased her about handcuffs did Deanna blush and go hot, but when this man said it, she wanted to kick him?

Maybe because she knew Justin wanted to play and to pleasure, to make her feel good. This guy didn't like women at all.

"I don't need the cuffs." Deanna stuck the barrel of the stun gun into his ribs. "If I squeeze this trigger, you'll be out for a couple of hours. Maybe longer. When you wake up, you'll be in a cell or maybe already on a transport. How long you're unconscious depends on what setting I have my stun gun on, and you know, I can't remember which it is now. So, you can either get off the Vistara and stay close to wherever you're billeting, or I stun you and process you. Your choice."

The man glanced at her gun, then at the passersby who were frowning at him, clearly on Deanna's side.

He took a step back but pointed his finger at her. "I'm reporting you, bitch."

"Please do. I'll be interested to hear my stationmaster's take on it."

With a final growl, the man turned on his heel and stalked off. He'd never looked again at Sybellie, which had been the whole point.

"You all right?" Deanna asked her.

Sybellie let out a shaky breath. "Remind me not to visit his planet, wherever it is."

"There's probably a sign posted to approaching craft—*Warning, assholes ahead.*"

Sybellie laughed, her mouth quirking in a way that reminded Deanna of Justin.

"Thank you for helping me," she said. "I wasn't quite sure what to do."

"You did fine. And never be afraid to call out for a patroller." Deanna glanced at the car where Justin waited. She couldn't see through the window, but she imagined Justin glued to the glass. "Would you like a ride somewhere? In case the guy doesn't clear out fast enough?"

Sybellie looked down the street, worried and hesitant at the same time. "If it's not too much trouble . . ."

"Not at all. It's my job to make sure citizens of Bor Narga are all right."

Sybellie let out another breath. "I'm on my way to the university."

"Easy. Come on." Deanna led the way around the car, opening the small back door for her.

When Deanna slid into the drivers' seat, Sybellie was settling herself in the back. Sybellie glanced curiously at Justin, who sat on the far side of his seat, against the door, looking poleaxed.

"Don't mind him," Deanna said as she sealed the doors and lifted the hovercar. "This is Justin. I'm giving him a ride too."

Chapter Twelve

Justin couldn't speak, couldn't think. Sybellie was sitting two feet from him, separated from him only by the seatback. Deanna calmly tapped controls to move the car quietly down the street, the air cooler kicking in to make the car a livable temperature.

Sybellie's hair was dark, her eyes a chocolate brown. She had Lillian's nose, but the shape of her mouth was Justin's. She wore the faintest scent, something powdery and lemony. It went with her, just like the rose-colored silks that whispered about her face.

"Is he all right?" Sybellie asked Deanna. "You haven't arrested him, have you?"

She was a Bor Nargan female, all right. Men were creatures of inferior intellect—so Bor Nargans believed—and women often talked about men in the room as though they weren't there.

"No, no," Deanna said. "I'm just giving him a lift."

Sybellie looked Justin over, as though trying to decipher what he was. "He doesn't look Bor Nargan. Where is he from?"

Justin opened his mouth to answer, but nothing came out. Every word he'd rehearsed to say to Sybellie if he ever met her jammed in his throat.

"He's from Sirius," Deanna said.

Sybellie looked interested, and she directed the next question at him. "I've never been there. What's Sirius like?"

She wasn't afraid of people, that was certain. But she'd probably never met anyone who'd been bad to her, excepting that jerk in the street.

Deanna answered, because Justin's mouth still wouldn't work. "There's lots of trees there, so I hear," Deanna said. "And meadows. And farms."

"Are you a farmer?" Sybellie asked Justin.

Justin cleared his throat. "No." He coughed, trying to open up his gullet.

"Well, they grow them tall on Sirius." Sybellie laughed, ingenuous and innocent. "Bor Nargan cars must be uncomfortable for you."

She doesn't know what I am. The words beat through Justin's head. *She doesn't know about Shareem.*

"Yes," he managed to say.

"Here's the university," Deanna said. "Which side of campus would you like?"

The far side, Justin willed. *It's too soon for you to go. Way too soon.*

"This is fine," Sybellie said, and Justin's heart ached. "Thank you for rescuing me."

Deanna set down the car and pushed a control to unseal the back door. "It was my pleasure. Believe me."

Sybellie sent her another smile, gathered her skirts and robes about her, and climbed out. She bent back through the door and directed her words at Justin.

"Good-bye. I hope you enjoy your stay on Bor Narga."

"Ungh," Justin said.

With one last radiant smile, Sybellie straightened up, turned with a swirl of silks, and walked off into the heat-shielded campus. An artificially generated breeze caught her skirts and veils as she waved at a group of approaching young women.

Deanna sealed the door against the heat and quietly turned the car around, heading down the street and back toward the main thoroughfare.

"Shit," Justin said. He passed a shaking hand over his face. "Shit, shit, shit, shit." He looked back, but the university was receding quickly, swallowed by buildings and hovercars. "What the holy fuck did you do that for?"

"You wanted to see her," Deanna said.

She looked so calm, tapping the controls to put the car on autopilot, programming it to take them back to Pas City. *Damn* her for looking so calm. Justin wanted to explode.

"Shit," he said again.

"I thought it was a good opportun—"

Her words cut off when Justin grabbed her, hauled her half out of her seat, and kissed her—hard.

"Justin, the car—"

"Is on autopilot."

He kissed her again, silencing her with his mouth. He dragged her up to him, licking and kissing.

Justin cupped her breasts through the coverall as she kissed him back, lifting them, full and warm. Her nipples became tight points under his thumbs, Deanna's intake of breath telling him she felt what he did.

He kissed his way down her throat as he ripped open the catch that held her coverall in place. He dragged the coverall down and pressed her upward to tongue the nipple that rose against her undertunic.

The car's console beeped. Deanna tried to extract herself, but Justin didn't care. He suckled her, tasting silk and the heat of her.

The console beeped again, more insistently. Justin's body did not want him to let her go, every nerve screaming with need for her. He wanted to fuck her right here in the car and damn the consequences.

"Justin, we'll wreck—"

Justin closed his teeth over her nipple before releasing her. Deanna grabbed the controls just in time to slide them into the narrow streets of Pas City.

Her coverall gaped open to her waist, the silk inside clinging to her breasts. Her hair was a mess, her face flushed, as she guided the craft along the street to stop in front of Justin's apartment.

"You're home," she said.

Justin reached over and killed the controls, and the car found the street with a thump.

"You're coming in with me," Justin said.

"No, I have to—"

He hit the controls, every door in the car opening. Justin locked his hands around Deanna and dragged her out with him through the passenger door to the bright, hot, empty street.

The car politely closed up again as soon as they were clear. Justin pulled Deanna to his rusty apartment door and palmed it open.

They nearly fell together into the apartment, and the door slammed closed behind them. Justin had Deanna against the wall, his body covering hers, before the door even hit the ground.

Deanna tried to stop him kissing her, tried to speak, but Justin didn't care. What she'd done . . . What she'd done for him . . .

He wanted to kiss and kiss her. Make love to her, play with her, and make love to her again.

He lifted her into his arms and carried her to the bedroom. The bed was rumpled, unmade from when

Justin had crawled out of it earlier, and Justin set Deanna squarely on it.

He pushed her open coveralls from her shoulders. Deanna made a token protest, but her eyes were warm, and she in the end helped pull the coverall from her body.

Her silken tunic clung to her, a nothing barrier between herself and him. One yank and it ripped, giving Justin access to her bare body.

Justin pulled and kicked his own clothes off, his skin itching to be out of them. He lowered himself on top of Deanna, and everything stopped.

He was breathing hard, and so was she. They looked at each other, gazes locking, Justin holding himself over her, neither of them moving.

Her skin was hot to the touch, warm with sweat, and Justin's body was scalding. In silence, he lowered his head to kiss her again, slowing down from his frenzied need.

Deanna parted her lips to take him. Their mouths met . . . and met again, slow in the midday heat. The sound of the kisses whispered in the room, the only touch in the silence.

Justin slid one hand to her breast, the supple cushion welcoming his hand. The point of her nipple poked between his first two fingers, and he rolled it as he kissed her, bringing it to beautiful tightness.

Deanna rested her arm on his shoulder, fingers finding and playing with his dark hair. Her eyes were languid brown, so dark he could drown in them. Justin kissed her lips once more before sliding his body down so he could feast on her breasts.

Justin suckled one breast as he cupped the other, caressing with fingers as much as he did with his tongue. He swirled around the areola before suckling again, loving the contrast between her silken skin, the cushion of the breast itself, and the tight apex of her nipple. When he finished, he moved to thoroughly taste and suck the other.

Deanna writhed as he worked her, her hands furrowing his hair. Justin kissed his way down her abdomen, licked her navel, then gently parted her thighs so that he could lie between them.

He studied her pussy as he ran his fingers down either side of her opening. Hers was a bit small, Deanna not a large-boned woman. But her entrance lay before him like a flower offering its petals, moist and inviting among her curled dark hair. Her clit was a little bud, pink and cute, beckoning his tongue.

Justin kissed the clit, then flicked his tongue on either side of her pussy. Deanna jumped, then her hips rose, her body begging for Justin to do what he wanted.

What *she* wanted. Justin closed his mouth over her, and drank.

Deanna thought she'd die. The room was hot, neither of them having stopped to turn on the cooler. Justin's apartment wasn't automated. Sweat dripped down her sides, but nothing was as wet as where Justin licked her.

His tongue moved in and out of her, or around the opening, or plunged inside, or closed with his mouth over her clit. The feeling was hot, wild, the friction driving her insane.

Justin's eyes were closed in concentration, his large hands on her hips. At one point he opened his eyes and looked up at her, the irises hot blue, obliterating the whites. She shivered at the so inhuman sight, but everything else about Justin was certainly all male.

She heard her voice ring through the room, without any realization that she'd cried out. The noises were sharp, animallike, and Deanna couldn't stop them.

"Justin! *Gods . . .*"

Then her words became incoherent, her cries shrill, as Justin took her on and on with his tongue.

And then it was over, her release complete. She fell onto the bed as though landing from a great height, trying to catch her breath.

But it wasn't over. Justin rose over her like a god, pressed her back into the bed with his large body, and entered her in one, long stroke.

No . . . she couldn't take it. He was so big. He'd tear her apart. And why did that excite her so much?

But he'd made her pussy wide and needy, and Deanna welcomed him in, spreading herself to take him.

Justin moved inside her swiftly, and in silence. His face was set, eyes that crazy blue, his mouth pressed together as he thrust and thrust.

He was trying to work something out of himself, and his cock was ramming into her to do it.

Deanna met his thrusts with her own, feeling her pussy squeeze around him, it somehow knowing what to do. But it was wonderful. She was hot from him drinking her, and the in-and-out friction of his cock wound her back to the wild place.

He started to grunt, his strong arms holding him off her as he thrust again and again. Deanna was crying out, the bed rocking, sweat drenching her body. His skin was slick under her fingers, his sweat dropping onto her like gentle rain.

Slippery and sliding, his cock pried her open, stretching her wide. She parted her thighs to take more of him, lifting her hips to bring him all the way inside her.

Justin grabbed her hip with one hand, pulling her up to him, showing her how. Deanna lifted her feet as he wound her thigh around him, wrapping her legs over his, pressing one sole to his buttocks.

Shareem cocks were twelve inches, one standard foot, and Justin's moved all the way inside Deanna. This wasn't pleasure, it was raw, mad, *fucking*, so crazy Deanna wanted it to last forever.

The world ceased to matter. Deanna knew nothing but the heat within her and without, the two of them rocking on the bed, Justin so deep inside her she knew nothing would ever satisfy her again.

But then they were both shouting, bodies slamming together, tears on Deanna's face. She seemed to be falling, falling, but his strong arms were there to catch her.

Deanna felt him come—his giant cock shot scalding seed far inside her, so much that she knew she'd never hold it.

But she did. He was glorious, and she'd never feel so fine and strong again.

"Deanna," he said, his voice harsh. "Thank you. Thank you."

He crashed onto her, his weight hot and hard, and all the wildness went out of him. He cradled her against him, open-mouthed kisses landing on her lips, her face, her hair.

"Thank you," he whispered brokenly.

Deanna touched his face, which was wet with tears. "You're welcome," she said.

*****

It occurred to Deanna, after some time, that underneath her was hard coolness, flooring designed to keep the heat at bay. The cool slab contrasted with Justin on top of her, and the heat of his mouth on her skin.

"When did we end up on the floor?" she asked.

"Don't remember." Justin pressed warm kisses along her breasts. "Don't care."

Deanna didn't much care either. It was beautiful here on the floor, with Justin on top of her. He was heavy, but he took care to not hurt her as he withdrew from her and rolled onto his side.

He made no suggestion that they get back on the bed but lay down next to her, spooning her against him, his hand finding her breast.

"Why did you do it?" he asked.

"Let you make love to me? I thought that was your idea."

"I mean let me see her so close."

Deanna shrugged, her body tired. "I didn't like to see you hurting."

She felt Justin's start, then he was up on his elbow, looking at her, stunned. "It was a wonderful gift, Deanna."

"Any time."

He let out a long breath and lowered himself to her side again, cradling her into his big body. "This isn't what I'm supposed to do. Fucking you like that, I mean."

"I don't know. It seemed fine to me. Not that I have any experience."

"I pleasure. I make you feel good. But this time, I couldn't stop myself. I had to *have you.*"

Deanna ran her hand across his callused fingers. "I have news for you. I felt good. I . . . well, I've never felt anything like it."

"I want to make you laugh, and beg, and laugh again." He wiped a tear from her lashes. "Not cry."

"I cried because it was beautiful," Deanna whispered.

Justin went silent, his head buried in the curve of her shoulder. She couldn't see his face in their position, but she felt his breath hot on her back.

He lay still for so long, that she thought he'd fallen asleep. Then he growled, a rumbling that vibrated, and the next thing she knew, he lifted her in his arms, up off the floor.

Back to the bed, this time side by side as they'd been on the floor, the mattress cushioning them. Justin got behind her, hooked his leg around hers, and moved her bent knee forward enough to open her to him. His cock, rock-hard again, pressed firmly against her backside, while he teased her opening, then he slid his cock into her pussy.

Deanna let out a long sigh that ended in a moan. Justin didn't thrust as much this time—he simply filled her, pressing farther and farther in with each smooth push.

It didn't take much until Deanna was coming again, her writhing pulling him deeper. Justin groaned under his breath, holding her in strong arms, his seed once more finding her.

He was still inside her when Deanna fell asleep, a profound, deep sleep that erased every fear and every dream. Here in the bed of a Shareem, she'd at last found contentment.

* * * * *

When Justin woke again, his body sore and sated, Deanna was gone. She wasn't in the shower—too bad—not in the living room waiting for him, not in the kitchen trying to scare up something to eat.

Justin pulled on his tunic and shoes, tied back his hair, and stepped outside into fading daylight. Maybe she'd gone to a vendors for some dinner. The gods knew Justin never had any food in the house.

The car was gone. Justin stopped, not liking how empty that made him feel. Logically, Deanna could have simply gone to return the car to wherever she'd hired it before she was charged for another day. Justin had been sleeping so hard that she might have shouted in his ears that she was going, and he'd never have heard.

But Justin knew somehow that she wouldn't be back tonight.

He went to the crowded marketplace around the corner, hoping against hope to see his patroller wandering among the stalls. He did see patrollers, two of them, buttoned up, hair in tight buns, but no Deanna.

"Justin."

Justin looked behind him to see an off-world man, taller than most Bor Nargan men, in a dusty pilot's coverall, his mussed hair light brown, his eyes deep green.

"Mitch," Justin grunted. "Didn't know you were back."

"Got here this morning. Rees is looking for you. And me."

Justin had no interest in talking to Rees right now, but he figured he might as well get it over with. "If you just got here this morning, why are you out here on the street and not inside doing Judith?"

"It's her busiest business time. Thought I'd give her a break."

"Nice of you."

"I'm a nice guy."

Mitch didn't break a smile as they started down the market street, whose artificial light glittered on tables filled with bright silks, cheap jewelry, fruits from all over the galaxy, piles of exotic spices, and shining mechanical parts. Women in everything from drab work-gray to silks as bright as the jewels they haggled for moved from stall to stall, the richer ones followed by servants who carried all the goods they bought.

"It's pretty here, in a weird way," Mitch said as they walked through the colorful chaos.

"Weird is right."

"Sirius is drab," Mitch said.

Yes, everyone wondered why Justin had returned to his native land, leaving the relative freedom of Sirius. Mitch was a laidback guy—very different from Bor Nargan men, even different from men on Sirius, who were pretty much into hard work, their idea of pleasure being one beer and a good night's sleep. Mitch would never directly ask Justin his reasons for returning, but Justin felt his curiosity.

"Come on," Justin said. "I bet Rees told us to haul our asses."

"True," Mitch said, finally grinning, and they walked on through the streets, until they reached the basement apartment where Rees lived with his lifemate.

Rees had lived here for years before he'd met Talan d'Urvey, his lady-love. Talan had a nice big house to herself on a nearby moon, but Rees and she stayed in the apartment when they were in Pas City. Talan seemed to like the tiny place for some reason.

Talan answered the front door. She was a diminutive woman with red hair, which she wore under a sheer veil, and a smile as warm as her heart.

She hugged Justin and gave him a kiss on his cheek, then greeted Mitch, without as much touchy-feely.

Talan led them through the tiny hall to the main room of the apartment. As they entered, Rees turned off whatever he was looking at on his computer and rose to greet them.

Chapter Thirteen

Rees was a bit taller than any of the Shareem, and larger too. He was a level three—or at least, that's what he told everyone.

Rees had been an experimental Shareem, a deep, dark secret kept by DNAmo, isolated from the others and put through some hellacious tests. Justin hadn't even known about Rees at DNAmo, not hearing about him at all until Justin's return to Bor Narga.

Rees was currently working on plans to take the Shareem off Bor Narga—permanently. Mitch had agreed to help, and Justin's part was to contact people he knew on Sirius to ready them for an influx of Shareem.

Except, Justin had asked Rees to postpone the exodus a while. Once the Shareem left Bor Narga, there was no coming back. Ever.

After the standard greetings—"How the hell've you been?" and shit like that, Rees got down to business.

"Who is this patroller that keeps following you around?" he asked Justin.

Justin bristled, protectiveness making him meet Rees's gaze with a hard one of his own. "Her name's Deanna." Justin flashed back to her underneath him on the floor, her breasts moving against him as he loved her. "She's all right."

"She's a patroller."

Rees's skeptical look was starting to piss him off. "She's smart and has compassion," Justin said. "Trust me, she's fine."

"You know we have to go soon. We only have so many windows of opportunity."

"I know."

Rees looked steadily at him, and Justin returned the stare without moving.

"What do you hear from Rio?" Mitch asked, breaking the tension.

Rio was the only Shareem who had ever escaped. He'd had the sense to run off with the daughter of the leader of Ariel, and was now immune from Bor Nargan persecution. Ariel was a fairly open planet, accepting of off-worlders, but they had a policy of letting in only a few new permanent residents per year, and the waiting list to get there was long.

However, Rio had resources that could help them go elsewhere.

"Rio says that Nella is lining up places we'll be safe on Station 475. If we get to Sirius and request asylum, from there, we can go anywhere."

"I've got guys to help with the transport," Mitch said. "But I don't want to give them too many details yet. And I can't guarantee they'll all be free at the same time."

Both men turned to look at Justin, who held up his hands. "I know you're waiting on me. It's taking longer to find Lillian than I thought, but I need to find her."

"Talan or Bree or Elisa can hire people here to look for her," Rees said. "She can be transported to wherever we end up."

"It's not that simple."

Rees went silent. Justin knew Rees was being patient with him and had said he understood about Sybellie, but Rees was right that they couldn't linger forever.

And now there was Deanna—the pretty patroller whose job it would be to stop Justin and the other Shareem leaving the planet. She'd be obligated to arrest him and line him up for execution for breaking one of the most basic laws Bor Nargans had about Shareem.

How could Justin justify endangering all Shareem to have a fling with a patroller? Or because he wanted to stay here and gaze at the daughter he loved?

He couldn't.

"Give me a few days," Justin said. "And I'll report what my contacts on Sirius say."

"Same here," Mitch said.

Rees gave them both a nod.

After a little more conversation—but not much, because it was clear that Rees wanted them gone—probably so he could screw Talan—Justin and Mitch departed together.

Mitch said little as they walked back toward Judith's, and that was fine with Justin. He had too many thoughts for conversation.

He could still feel Deanna's warmth around him, could still scent her desire. To help the Shareem stuck on this planet, Justin would have to turn his back on her, and on Lillian, and Sybellie.

Break a Shareem's heart.

He looked at Mitch. "Want to help me find an off-worlder who pissed me off today?"

"Sure. What did he do?"

"Was rude to a lady."

Deanna had driven off the asshole, but Justin still wanted to kill him. *Put your hands on my daughter, and see what happens to you . . .*

"Are you saying the lady didn't have him arrested? This is Bor Narga."

"Long story. I'd like to find him, and explain how I feel about it."

Mitch grinned. "Let's do it."

One thing Justin liked about Mitch—the man didn't demand explanations or waste time arguing. He simply started walking with Justin through the narrow streets toward the space docks and the lodgings for off-worlders there.

Only the very richest and most important off-worlders were allowed to stay up on the hill, and the guy had looked neither rich nor important. So it was an even bet he'd found a place to stay in the off-world quarter.

Justin figured that finding the guy was a long shot, but even looking for him made Justin feel better. But then, the man had been an arrogant jerk, and arrogant jerks were bad at keeping low profiles.

Sure enough, in the fourth bar Mitch and Justin visited, Justin saw the man who'd accosted his daughter.

The man still wore his dark coverall, and he was being rude to the woman behind the bar. The woman was getting ready to throw his ass out.

Justin and Mitch went to lean on the bar on either side of him. Mitch drawled at the bartender, "Want us to take out the garbage, darlin'?"

The bartender shrugged. "Fine by me. Just don't bring patrollers down on me," she added with a sharp look at Justin.

The man was too full of himself to understand what was happening until Justin and Mitch seized him between them and dragged him toward the door.

"What the fuck?" The man tried to struggle, but he was too drunk, the pair of them too strong.

Justin and Mitch half-carried him into the alley around the corner and threw the man up against a wall. The alley was dark, strewn with garbage and sand, the smell thick.

"Fine, I'll go to another bar," the man said sulkily. "I didn't like that shithole anyway."

"We're not the bouncers," Justin said. "I'm the friend of someone you upset today."

"Yeah?" The man frowned, as though sifting through all the people he'd upset that day and wondering which one they meant. "Who the hell are you?" He looked Justin up and down. "*What* the hell are you? You're not Bor Nargan."

"Bor Nargan born and bred," Justin said. "And really unhappy with you."

"Well, you don't look like the little pussy men who live here. If one of them was your fuckhole, and I made him cry, I don't care." The man's frown cleared. "Or maybe it was the pretty little piece up in the rich town. She your whore? Tell you what, why don't you let me take a poke with her, and we'll forget the whole thing—"

Justin's punch caught him in the gut, and the man's breath whooshed out of him. Drunk *and* stupid.

Justin punched and kept on punching. The man started to defend himself, fists returning blows, which Justin deftly blocked. Shareem weren't supposed to be fighters, but Justin had learned fighting out of necessity on the docks of Sirius.

He blocked and hit, catching the man in the jaw, the face, the gut again. The man fought back somewhat skillfully, in spite of his inebriation, but Justin was sober and very experienced.

Mitch never jumped in to help, seeming to understand that Justin needed to do this, even if he didn't know exactly why.

Justin balled his fist and landed one last, practiced punch to the man's face. The off-worlder's head snapped back, then his eyes rolled closed, and he slid down the wall. Nice.

Justin shook out his hand. "We're done here," he said, out of breath.

"Remind me not to piss you off," Mitch said, leading the way out of the alley.

"I will." Justin caught up to him. "Now, let's go get drunk."

* * * * *

Deanna's mother was having a bad night. She couldn't eat, couldn't sit still, and couldn't stop moaning. Deanna and Reda did everything they could, but in the end, Reda ended up tranquilizing her.

Deanna brushed back her mother's hair as her face relaxed with the tranq. "I'm sorry, Mama," she whispered, kissing her cheek.

"Pretty soon, I won't be able to look after her by myself," Reda said, putting away the tranq box. "Oh, don't look like that, honey. It's not that I don't want to, but I don't have training at that level. And she'll need more than one person to help her, full time."

"I know."

Deanna folded her arms tightly over her chest. A few hours ago, she'd felt so wonderful in Justin's bed, curled back against him, falling asleep with him still inside her. She'd loved to have stayed all night, but she'd needed to return the car and check on her mother and Reda.

Problems with her mother tonight had brought it home to Deanna that she needed to make things right in her job. She had to keep on getting paid, keep receiving the compensation for her mother's care. If her mother had to go to fulltime care, that would be even more expensive. Deanna had gotten a settlement from the space station where her mother had stumbled into the radiation repair, but it still wasn't enough.

And, Deanna missed her mother. The warmhearted woman who'd raised her was gone, a stranger in her place.

The sooner Deanna helped Justin find Lillian, the sooner Deanna could get him out of her life and return to normal.

Normal. Sure.

Deanna helped Reda make Kayla comfortable in bed, then Deanna went back to her computer to follow up on her search for Lillian.

After another hour, Deanna was pretty sure she was right about what she'd come up with. At least, it was worth a trip to find out.

She brought up her communications function and called Justin. No answer.

She called him again half an hour later. And again. And again.

Justin either wasn't home or wasn't answering — all night — for whatever reason.

This was too important, though, to worry that he was avoiding her. She shut down her computer, told Reda she was going out, and headed back to the heart of Pas City as the sky was lightening to gray.

* * * * *

"I'm closed," the red-haired bartender said. She was clinking glasses and metal tankards behind the bar, shoving them through her sterilizer.

Deanna glanced at the off-worlder who sat on a barstool, a glass of ale in front of him. He'd had a few, by the look of him, but he managed to pin Deanna with a steady stare.

He had green eyes, almost emerald in color, startling on a world of dark-eyed people. Deanna had done her research—his name was Mitch and he liked to frequent this bar when he was on Bor Narga.

"I'm not a customer," the man said. The fact that he answered for himself, instead of letting a woman do it, also marked him as an off-worlder. "I'm a friend."

"All my paperwork is in order," Judith the bartender said. "And I'm too busy for a spot inspection. Come back tomorrow."

Deanna held up her hands. "I'm off duty. I came to find Justin."

Judith didn't stop messing with the glasses. "He lives next door."

"I know that. He won't answer his door."

Judith shrugged. "Then he wants to be left alone. He's had enough trouble with patrollers."

Deanna drew a breath, trying to stem her impatience. "I need to see him. I'm helping him with something." She glanced again at the green-eyed man. "I'm a friend," she echoed his words.

The man's interest perked. "Wait a minute. Did a dickhead off-worlder make your life hell sometime today?"

Deanna remembered the asshole on the Vistara, and the satisfaction she'd taken in making him walk away.

"Yes, but I took care of it. Why?"

The man grinned. "I'd say Justin took care of it. It was a thing of beauty."

"What was?" Deanna asked in alarm. "What did he do?"

"I didn't know Shareem could fight like that."

Fight like what? *"What did he do?"*

"Found the guy and beat him up for you. I got to watch." The man chuckled.

"Why didn't you stop him?" Deanna demanded. "He's going to get himself arrested." She trailed into muttering. "Damn it."

"Why do you want to see him?" Judith asked.

"I have to tell him something important. He's been dodging my calls all night, and now he won't answer the door."

"He was pretty drunk when we parted company," Mitch said.

Judith finally looked up from her cleaning and studied Deanna, but she directed her words at Mitch. "I think she's the patroller Justin was talking about.

Aiden said he saw them together the other day, going into Justin's apartment."

"The one Justin says looks hot in her coveralls?" Mitch answered, giving Deanna a once-over. "I'm willing to bet."

Deanna's face heated. "I really need to talk to him."

"So, go talk to him," Judith said.

Deanna blew out her breath. Justin's door was locked, he wouldn't take her calls, and from what Mitch had said, he might be drunkenly asleep.

Then again, Deanna was still a patroller, and she had a pass code to override his door if necessary. And she had handcuffs.

She looked at Judith then Mitch, who both watched her expectantly. She nodded. "All right."

Deanna turned around and walked back out into the coming dawn.

Chapter Fourteen

Justin was having a bad dream.

He was at DNAmo again, his hands and feet bound, while the scientists injected him with everything from suped-up adrenaline to the strongest tranquilizers to see what his system could take. He remembered his heart nearly exploding in his chest and him screaming, to being so groggy he barely had strength to breathe.

If he doesn't make it, one of the scientists was saying, *take a few DNA samples and incinerate the body.*

Kind of a waste, another said.

Don't worry. He has a daughter. We can do the tests on her.

No!

Justin jerked his hands as he came awake, panting and sweating, and found his wrists still bound together.

What the fuck?

He lay facedown on his bed, naked—he'd stripped off his clothes before he'd fallen onto the mattress and never bothered with the covers. His arms were now stretched over his head, his wrists tethered to his headboard.

The cuffs felt wrong, though. They weren't the super-strong metal that had kept him constrained at DNAmo, but soft and warm, like his own toys.

Someone had gotten out his handcuffs and manacled him to his own bed.

Justin lifted his head, his headache pounding as he looked over his shoulder.

He went instantly hard when he saw Deanna standing beside his bed, arms folded, her coverall half open to reveal the tunic beneath.

"What the fuck?" he said out loud. Or maybe he should say, *be gentle with me, sweetheart.*

Then again, he didn't want any gentleness going on in this room right now. Rough play had its time, and that time was now.

"You didn't answer your com," Deanna said. "Or your door."

"Busy. Then drunk."

"And sound asleep. You never heard me come in."

"Are you arresting me? Again? Have to admit, this is more fun than the first time. Or do you have a stun gun ready to go?"

"I should," Deanna said. "But I don't." She put her hand on his bare shoulder, and Justin jumped like he'd been shocked. "I was thinking about a dream I had after I met you. I dreamed I came into your apartment, and you were tied to a chair, waiting for me."

Justin got harder. "Yeah? You have a thing for putting me in bondage, do you Patroller?"

"Maybe." Deanna's voice was soft. "Though I don't know why."

"You're a closet dominatrix?"

"I don't even know what that means."

"You like being in control," Justin said. "You want to be the one holding the whip, so to speak. Maybe that's why you became a patroller."

"I don't know." Again the soft wonder. "I like both ways, I think."

Justin broke into a warm sweat. "That's what a level two likes to hear."

Deanna reached for the bedside table, and he realized that his box of accoutrements lay open on it. His heart beat faster as she lifted something out of it.

"What are these?" She showed him the three small balls nestled in their velvet-lined box.

"Those are for you. To remind you of me when I'm not around. Want me to show you how to use them?"

"Not yet." Deanna returned the box, to his disappointment, and brought out a slim, small plug. "What is this?"

"Ass plug."

"Do you use it on yourself?"

"Sometimes."

"Why?"

Why? Why bother to eat delicious food when bland fare will keep you alive?

Justin shrugged the best he could. "It feels good. Full. Stimulating. Want me to show you?"

Deanna examined the little plug in curiosity. It wasn't very big, just enough to feel, to enhance the lady's pleasure while he pleasured her in other places. "How does it . . ? How do you . . . ?"

"Lube. In the jar. Smear it on, and it goes in nice."

He held his breath while Deanna opened a jar of flowery-smelling lube and tentatively smeared it on the plug. Watching her concentrate, the toy near her face, had him throbbing and ready.

Justin pulled at his cuffs, but they wouldn't budge. He'd designed them himself, and he'd done a good job.

Deanna put the lube away, then her lips quirked into a little smile as she touched the plug to Justin's buttocks. "It goes here?"

Justin stiffened. She didn't mean she wanted to try it on herself. Oh, no. His little patroller preferred to torture Justin.

He forced himself to relax. "You have to play a little bit. Get me ready and open. It's a very sensitive place, and it can hurt if you rush."

"I won't hurt you, Justin."

Gods, hearing her say that in her sexy little voice was going to make him lose it way too soon.

"Put lube on your fingers. Then touch me there, very gently, until I open to you."

Deanna nodded, her expression solemn. He might be instructing her how to fix a hovercar.

He watched while she opened the lube again, making her fingers glisten. When she lowered her hand to his backside, Justin closed his eyes and moved all his attention to the warm, sensual pressure of her fingers.

She had no idea what to do. An experienced woman would press around his entrance before slipping in a finger. Deanna touched, caressed, rubbed, and played, until Justin thought he'd come off the bed.

This was so backward. *He* should be tethering her, touching her, teaching her how to take the plug. But how sexy was it to teach her how to pleasure him, and how fucking good it was to lie here and take it.

Under her silken touch, his cock got harder, his backside more ready. The warmth of her fingertip slipped inside—by her start, she hadn't expected that. But she'd learn that when it was time, it was time.

"Now," he whispered.

He clenched his jaw when her warm, sweet finger went away, then made himself relax again when he felt the cooler press of the plug. It slid in, nice and snug, not too big.

"What does that feel like?" Deanna asked, full of curiosity.

"Hot. Full. Satisfying. Good. I'll show you once you unlock me."

She didn't move to. "What else can I do to you?"

Justin's headache had disappeared. His body was pliant, warm, excited. "Turn me over and suck me. Let me suck you. Get up here in front of me so I can fuck you. Want me to go on?"

Her eyes went wide at his blunt words, but she stood her ground. "How could you . . . back to front?"

Justin leveraged himself to his knees, the plug staying put. He held on to the headboard, his cock sticking out like a thick pole.

"There's plenty of room for you to kneel in front of me, even if you did chain me up."

"You mean . . . up my ass?"

The hesitant way she said it had him throbbing with longing. "No, sweetheart. That's too much for you yet. I mean in your pretty pussy. I can do you if you're in front of me."

She wanted to. Her cheeks and throat were flushed, her nipples tight. Justin waited for her to turn and walk out, to leave him manacled and needy, to have second thoughts about being here at all.

Then she pulled her coverall down and stripped out of her underclothes. Naked, she was sleek and beautiful, her breasts full, hips curved, legs strong.

Still, Deanna hesitated, hands pressed together, fingertips at her mouth.

"I'm your prisoner, Deanna Surrell," Justin said, his need for play rising. "What do you want your prisoner to do?"

Deanna swallowed, her slender throat moving. All at once, she ducked under his arm and came up on the bed, facing him.

"This," she said, and kissed him.

* * * * *

Deanna shook all over as Justin kissed her, his strong mouth pinning her despite his hands being cuffed.

Touching him had been exciting, watching him respond to her had made her feel powerful and tender at the same time.

Before when he'd loved her, he'd started slowly, caressing. This time, his mouth punished, his teeth catching and nipping her lips. "Turn around," he said.

"I thought I was the one calling the shots," Deanna said.

"Turn around and take hold of the headboard, before I break out of my chains and swat your ass."

Deanna shivered, a dark excitement rushing through her. She kissed his lips one more time, then obeyed.

She wasn't certain that there was room, but Justin told her how to get positioned in front of him, her back to him, hips canted up and open to him. She jerked when his tip pressed her opening . . . no, he wouldn't fit.

Before Deanna could slide away in worry, Justin pushed himself all the way inside.

He was filling her up, spreading her, too much, too much. Having him inside her the first time had felt good, but this took her breath away.

"You like that, Deanna?" he asked. "Sweet baby. You like being full of me?"

"Yes. *Yes.*"

"You're a cute little tease." Justin's hands were strong on the headboard, his forearms bunching with muscle. "Binding my hands, playing with my ass. I can't let you get away with that."

"No," she said breathlessly.

"So take me. Take all of me."

She was taking all of him, whether she liked it or not—and she decided she definitely liked it.

"I'm only sorry I can't spank your ass while I'm doing you," Justin said. "But you have me chained. Later, though, I'll make up for it."

Spank her? Deanna wasn't sure what to think of that. But Justin thrusting against her, his balls slapping her ass, made a pleasant tingle on her skin.

He kept thrusting, never slowing, never backing off the power. Deanna lost control of her words, crying out how much she loved what he was doing to her. Justin's dark voice responded, calling her his, telling her what he wanted to do to her, how much he loved fucking her.

It went on until Deanna was certain nothing in her life had ever existed but this bed beneath her hands and knees, the strong man thrusting into her and making himself a part of her. Fire ignited where they joined and ran through her body, the stream of it one, and whole.

"Deanna. Gods. *Fuck.*"

Justin's seed scalded into her, as Deanna continued to come apart. She wanted to cry, the feeling so beautiful, knowing that it wouldn't last.

She heard the sound of tearing metal, then Justin's hands were on her back, his weight pressing her down into the bed.

He started to laugh, his breath hot in her ear. Justin caressed her hair, turning her head so he could kiss her, still laughing. The chain had broken, Justin's hands still in the wide cuffs, but no longer tethered together around the headboard.

Deanna laughed too, loving how his body shuddered on top of hers. He was still inside her, still hard, but they moved more slowly together, until they drifted to silence. Justin's bedside clock chimed softly to show that it was full morning, the sun up now, the last thing Deanna heard before she drifted to sleep.

* * * * *

Justin had a momentary panic when he opened his eyes again. The last time he'd fallen asleep with Deanna, she'd been gone when he awoke, and he'd lain there, bereft. He hadn't liked that feeling, didn't want to experience it again.

But Deanna was stretched out next to him, breathing softly, and he relaxed in relief.

Justin must have slid out of her in his sleep, and now he nestled behind her, his thigh firmly pressing her rump. The butt plug was still in him, though. He reached around and carefully worked it out, then leaned across Deanna to drop it into the sterilizer on the other side of his nightstand.

Deanna turned her head and looked at him sleepily as he eased back onto the bed.

Justin kissed her shoulder. "Hey," he said.

"Hey." She was so beautiful with her dark hair tangled over her body, her brown eyes warm. "Why do you always do that?"

"Make hard love to you? Because you're gorgeous, sexy, and a real sweetheart. How can I stop myself?"

"I mean why do you always distract me? I came over here to tell you something."

Justin smiled as he licked across her shoulder. "Why didn't you wake me up and tell me then?"

"Because when I saw you . . . it made me think of my dream. I couldn't resist."

"I'm glad I led you into temptation then." Justin slid his fingers under her breast, lifting the weight of it. "I'd happily do it again."

"I really do have something important to tell you."

"Better tell me then, before I wake up all the way. Because I'm going to want to distract you again."

Justin was drowsy, sated for the first time in ages, but her next words wiped away his warmth.

"I think I know where Lillian is."

Justin stopped, hand firming on her breast. She watched him in some trepidation but also determination.

"I told you to leave that the hell alone," Justin said. "Remember?"

"And I told you I could help. I can get into databases that are closed to most people, even your librarian friend—I assume she was helping you look up Lillian that day I saw you coming out of the library. Don't you want to know what I found out?"

Justin did, and at the same time, he wanted Deanna to have nothing to do with this. Knowledge was dangerous. "Yes," he said tersely.

"I used the DNA tracer to locate a person with an exact match to the DNA I found on your veil. The tracer picked up Lillian's old records, and then the records of another person with a different name."

Justin stilled. "Who? Where is this person?"

"I don't know."

"Damn it, Deanna, you just said . . ."

"I'll explain if you let me finish." She raised up on one elbow and pushed her hair back from her face. "The record I found is about fourteen years old, and there aren't any after that. But I know Lillian never left the planet. Even if she stowed away and got off planet, there would be a DNA record of her *somewhere*. She'd have to apply for housing or for a job, and she'd have to give a DNA sample. You can change your name and where you live, but you can't change your DNA."

Justin lay silently, barely able to breathe. Elisa's searches for Lillian too had not shown her on any other planet. Even if Lillian had died, the DNA of the deceased would be registered, regardless of what name she'd been using.

"So what are you saying?" Justin asked. "Were the records wiped after that? And how?"

Deanna shook her head, the ends of her hair brushing Justin's skin. "I've thought of the only explanation that fits. There is one group of people on Bor Narga allowed to hide all record of themselves, allowed to be completely anonymous, untouchable even by the rulers. It's very, very hard to get accepted into their enclaves, but once Lillian became one of them, her records would be closed and unsearchable."

"What group?" Justin had lived most of his life off Bor Narga — thank the gods — and he couldn't place what she was talking about. "She became one of who?"

Deanna took a breath. "The celibate orders. I think Lillian joined one of the Ways. She's taken the robes and gone into seclusion, which means that all record of her can vanish without a trace."

* * * * *

Justin got them up and out in record time. Deanna saw the agitation in him, the desperation, even as they both showered and dressed.

"Where are we going?" she asked as Justin all but shoved her out the door ahead of him. "I don't know which order she's in, or where. Like I said, the records are sealed, even to me."

"We're going to see someone who knows all about the celibate orders," Justin said striding ahead of her to lead the way.

He took her out through the immense, bright heat of the morning to the street on which she'd spied him before, when he'd gone to the small library that served citizens of this part of Pas City.

The library was more crowded than she'd have thought, with people on every console, and others asking questions of the librarians. A year ago, this place had been almost deserted.

Justin went to a counter and leaned his arms on it, waiting for a pretty woman in a light robe and tastefully draped veils to finish helping the person she was talking to. *Highborn*, Deanna classified her. Working here because she wanted to, not because she needed the job.

The woman turned after the last patron left her desk, and her eyes widened as she glanced from Justin to Deanna. "Hello, Justin. Is anything wrong?"

"We need to talk. Can we . . . ?" He made a vague gesture at the door behind her.

The librarian nodded, turned on a sign that told people to go to the next librarian on the counter, and led Justin and Deanna through the door to a small, cool room in the back. Deanna heard soundproofing click into place when the door slid shut.

Justin started to speak, but the librarian held out her hand to Deanna. "I'm sorry, we haven't been introduced."

Definitely highborn. Only someone from the Serestine Quarter would demand that manners be followed no matter how dire the situation.

Deanna, as the lower-ranking woman in the room, went first. "Deanna Surrell, Patroller First Class."

"Elisa n'Arell, Library Director."

She came from an old and rich family, Deanna surmised, with a name like that and veils that would cost Deanna a month's pay.

"I'm not arresting Justin, if that's what you're worried about," Deanna said.

"She already did that," Justin said. "She likes handcuffs. And other things."

Elisa looked at both of them again, took in Justin's half-grin, and made an "oh" of understanding. Deanna blushed harder than she had in her life.

"You can stop explaining right there, Justin," Elisa said. "I don't need to know. But you're frothing at the mouth about something. What?"

"Lillian joined a celibate order," Justin said. "I want to know which one."

Elisa looked surprised. "An order? You're sure?"

Deanna answered. "It's the only explanation. I've been helping Justin try to find her," she added at Elisa's continued surprise.

"Order records are sealed," Elisa said. "Even to me." She peered at Deanna. "Are you *very* sure?"

"Very. It's the only way all records of her after a certain point could disappear. Even DNA records. I found reference to her new name when I did a DNA search, but only one. Then . . . nothing."

"Yes, you could be right." Elisa's eyes took on a keen light, as though she'd enjoy sifting through all the data again herself. "It never occurred to me she might have joined an order—they're very selective. I was going on with looking for a name change or move off planet, and I have no access to the DNA records. But even if what you say is true, I can't get into order records."

"But you know people," Justin said. "If I believe everything Braden says, you were pretty high up in your Way. You'd know who to ask. Ask them."

Deanna's world was sure being shoved around this week. A Shareem, classified as the lowest of sentient life forms on Bor Narga, was sitting here demanding that a highborn woman formerly from a celibate Way use her contacts to help him. He wasn't groveling or even asking politely. Justin looked highborn Elisa n'Arell straight in the eye and told her to help him, and Elisa didn't even blink.

"It's a good idea, Justin, but I can't promise anything," Elisa said. "Some of the orders can be very close-mouthed."

Justin's grin spread over his handsome face. "You'll sweet-talk them, Elisa, as only you can."

And now the highborn woman was blushing. "I'll try."

"Thank you." Justin rose, but instead of giving the woman a polite nod or bow as lower-ranking people were supposed to, he cupped her shoulders and kissed her on the cheek. "Tell Braden to be extra special to you."

Her smile warmed her eyes. "I'll do that."

Justin led Deanna back outside. The heat had pumped up as the sun moved to its zenith, and sweat trickled between Deanna's shoulder blades.

"Was she ever . . ." Deanna cleared her throat and forced out the question. "Was she one of your clients?" The comfortable way Justin had spoken to Elisa, coupled with the kiss, which Elisa had accepted while blushing rosy red, pointed that way. The level of jealousy this gave Deanna dismayed her.

"Elisa? No, she's Braden's girl—remember I told you that when you asked me what I was doing here the last time?" Justin stopped and pulled her to face him. The Bor Nargan sun made his still-wet hair glisten, and shadowed his tanned skin. "Or did you think I went to the library that day to see her for sex?"

Deanna tried to shrug. "Of course that's what I thought. You're Shareem."

"I can see that we need to have a little talk."

Justin took her hand and almost dragged her back through the streets toward his apartment.

Instead of leading her inside, though, Justin ducked with her into the bar next door.

"I see you found him," Judith said from behind the counter.

Deanna's face went hot, but Justin pulled her past Judith, and Mitch, who sat on his usual stool at the bar.

"We're taking the corner table," Justin said. "Keep everyone away, but bring the ale. Deanna and I need to talk."

"Uh-oh," Mitch said.

Judith wiped her hands, pulled taps to dispense two tankards of ale, and brought them to the table. "Be nice to her, Justin," Judith said. "Patrollers can't help being what they are."

Justin shook his head. "Deanna's a good lady. Don't worry."

Judith raised her brows but walked away without a word, back to the bar and Mitch.

Deanna took a sip of ale, finding it surprisingly good, but Justin didn't drink.

"I'm Shareem," Justin said, his blue eyes steady. "But I left Bor Narga a long time ago and lived like a real human being. I got together with a woman and stayed with her in a permanent relationship. Shela and I were together, with no one else. Occasionally, we'd bring in a third or a fourth, but only for fun, and only briefly."

Deanna coughed, wiped her mouth, and set down her tankard. "A third or a *fourth*?"

"Yes." No explanation, no embarrassment, just the one word. "When I moved back to Bor Narga, Elisa and Braden were going through some things. I was their third a couple of times, but it was for fun only, to help them work out their problems. They've invited me back once or twice, but lately, I haven't been interested."

"No?"

"No." Justin leaned to her, his gaze intense. "Because I'm more interested in a patroller with pretty eyes."

"Oh." Deanna swallowed and started to say more, but he cut her off.

"I'm not finished. DNAmo created Shareem to be living pleasure toys—played with until the lady is bored then handed off to the next lady in line. But the reality is that Shareem like to be with certain people, and not others, and they can fall in love. I wasn't smart enough to hide that with Lillian at DNAmo, which is why they broke us up. On Sirius, I got with Shela, and we were very happy. And now, I'm finally finding something like happiness again with you, which means I'm not running around fucking every woman in sight. All right?"

Deanna listened, heart pounding. The way he looked at her made her warm and happy, and she couldn't quite make her tongue start working again.

"All right?" Justin repeated, waiting.

She nodded quickly and cleared her throat. "I believe you."

"You clinched it when you handcuffed me to the bed." Justin's smile glimmered through. "Nice touch.

I was trying to convince myself that I couldn't possibly feel anything for a patroller, and then you went and excited me more than I've been excited in a long time, and now you're helping me find Lillian. Why?"

That was easy. "Because I hate seeing you so sad. Because I know why you need to find her. Because I don't think it's fair what they did to you."

Justin watched her closely, eyes so deeply blue in his handsome face. "You're sweet, Patroller."

"I'm not sweet." Deanna balled her fists. "I just . . . I thought you'd be different. I never realized how much I'd like you."

"Fair dues," Justin said. "I never thought I'd like you. And then you go and make me care."

"So what do we do?"

Justin started to smile. "Have more sex?"

"Is that your answer to everything?"

"It is what I am. No matter how we feel inside, Shareem still like sex, and we like to explore every sexual facet we can. That's why some add the third — or fourth, or fifth — to enjoy the spice."

"Is that what you want to do with me?" Deanna unclenched her hands and laced them around her ale glass. "Add more people?"

"No, actually. I'm finding that I don't want to share you. But there's other ways we can play. Like more of what we've done, or watching, or . . ."

"Wait, wait. Watching? Watching what? You mean like . . . dirty vids?"

Justin let out a laugh. "Vids are boring. There's nothing like watching a passionate couple really into each other. They know you're watching, and they like it, which makes it even more hot."

Deanna felt her mouth drop open. "If you say so."

"And if we get so into it that we rip off each other's clothes and start in ourselves, all the better."

"In *front* of them? You're crazy, right?"

"It can be fun, Deanna, with the right people. If everyone's consenting, what the hell?"

"Do you do this often?"

Justin looked surprised. "No. Like I said, it has to be the right couple and the right time. You're adventurous, sweetheart. I see that in you. I think you'd enjoy the experience. But if you don't want to." He shrugged. "Fine by me. There's plenty other things that are fun."

"You *are* crazy."

But Deanna wondered. Would she feel horribly embarrassed seeing two people making love to each other, or would it spur her—especially if Justin was next to her—to want it too? Pheromones were unpredictable things.

Even so, such an idea was out of her realm. *Justin* was out of her realm.

"I'm not sure about that," Deanna said.

"Don't worry. I said, I have many ideas."

"Once you find Lillian, though . . ."

"Once I find Lillian, what?"

She wasn't certain. If Lillian was in a celibate order, Justin couldn't run off with her, but what would he and Lillian decide to do? They'd been something to each other once, and they shared a child.

"Justin, what we have can't possibly go anywhere," she said in a rush.

"I was thinking the same thing, actually, until you broke into my house this morning and chained me up."

"I know I did, but . . ."

"Now, I'm willing to think about it. I'm ready to let what happens, happen. I learned a long time ago not to throw something away because other people try to screw it up for you. What I have with you is none of anyone's business."

"But it's dangerous for both of us," Deanna said. "You don't know everything about me, Justin. Anything, really. My mother . . ." She studied her ale, then decided it better to meet his gaze as she explained. "My mother is very ill. Incurably, they tell me."

Chapter Fifteen

The sudden compassion on Justin's face surprised her. "Gods, Deanna. I'm sorry. What happened?"

Deanna told him briefly while he listened, still with that compassion. "And there's really nothing that can be done?" he asked when she finished.

Deanna shook her head. "I've looked into every treatment. There might be something off-world I don't know about, but anything I've found that might help even a little is so hideously expensive, I couldn't possibly save up enough for it in time . . . And I won't try some strange experimental treatment that might make her worse."

"I wish you'd told me," Justin said.

"Why?" Deanna asked sharply. "Would you have left me in peace?"

"No, I would have tried to help you sooner. I have resources you don't know about."

"What resources? What are you talking about?"

"People. Knowledge. Money."

"I looked you up, Justin. I learned every last thing about you. You don't have money. You have a house on Sirius, but it's sitting empty. And I know who you know. If you mean Katarina d'Arnal, your medic friend, she's not qualified to treat profound chemical problems like this one."

"Databases only cough up what people put into them, doesn't matter how good your clearance code is," Justin said. "If the database doesn't know about it, no one can find out about it."

"Meaning you're keeping secrets from the Bor Nargan government?"

"Yes."

"Good." Deanna lifted her ale and took a nice, long drink.

Justin grinned. "See? You're not so bad. I'll make some inquiries and let you know. In the meantime . . ."

"In the meantime?" Deanna's heart beat faster. She didn't think he could help her — the situation was beyond help — but she liked that he wanted to.

"In the meantime, I think we should do what you suggested and have more sex."

Deanna felt her mouth move into a smile. She looked into his eyes, which had scared her and fascinated her the first time she'd seen them. "Maybe you're right," she said.

* * * * *

Justin thrust again, liking how her eyes half-
closed whenever he slid all the way inside her. And
she made such delicious little noises.

"I love fucking you," Justin said. "Just fucking,
no games."

"Yes . . ."

Justin held on to his bed frame and thrust again,
she face-up under him, the sweat between their bare
bodies slick and hot. She smelled good, womanly
musk and salt.

"You're tight," he whispered. "You're making
me come again. Damn it, I'm not ready."

Deanna gave him a languid smile and *squeezed*.
The little sweetheart had learned her lessons well.

"Deanna," he said as his mind blanked to
everything but her. "Deanna. *Gods*."

Her own cry joined his as Deanna peaked, her
body moving in rhythm under his. "Justin," she
groaned. "Justin, *I love you*."

* * * * *

The room went silent as they wound down.
Deanna's face was relaxed in passion, but her eyes
held trepidation, almost fear.

Justin kissed her, the warm, slow kisses of
afterglow. "Shh."

"Justin . . ."

"No," he whispered. "Don't take it back. Don't,
sweetheart."

Deanna bit her lip, and Justin pulled her close. He felt the shudder of her breath, her fears, everything that was between them.

They lay together for a long time, he still inside her. He knew he'd missed his window of opportunity to get himself to the Vistara and see Sybellie, but he'd forgo that for one day.

Right now, he needed to be with Deanna. Even though he knew rough times would come, especially in light of Rees wanting to get them off planet, he hadn't liked Deanna's declaration that they couldn't have anything beyond this. He wanted this, and so much more.

For now, he could hold her, drink in the scent of her, and let himself bask in just being with her.

And play with her. After a time, when he knew she'd rested enough, he murmured, "You made me come too soon, little darling."

"*I* did? How?"

"By being your sweet self. And squeezing like I taught you."

"Like this?" She gave a little squeeze, and Justin went rock hard again.

"Damn you, woman. Just for that . . ."

He pulled out, much as he hated to, and had her on her stomach before she could fight him. His velvet-lined cuffs were ready, and he locked them around her outstretched wrists. She wriggled and cried out in protest.

"There," he said. "How do you like being on the receiving end?"

"Justin."

Justin locked the handcuffs together around the headboard with a slim chain. "Hmm, this looks familiar. Except it was me with my ass in the air."

"You let me go right now," Deanna said, but not very convincingly. "I'm a patroller."

"That's true. A patroller who's been very, very bad. Sleeping with Shareem, playing with toys."

As he spoke, Justin reached for the oil that he'd had Aiden mix for him, the one that smelled of jasmine. He opened the bottle, the heady aroma filling the air, and dribbled oil onto her back.

She jumped. "What are you doing? Oh, that smells good."

And because Aiden, the best level one ever, had mixed it, the oil had soothing pheromones in it as well. A concoction to make a woman relaxed, happy, and needy.

Justin smoothed the oil down her back and over her buttocks. Deanna stretched and purred.

"This is the nice part," Justin said. "Level twos get to be a little bit level one." He lifted his hand away. "And a little bit level three."

He let his hand come down—*smack*—on her ass.

Deanna jumped and yelped. Justin spanked her a few more times, then rested his tingling hand on her warmed buttocks. "That's for tying me down. Which I liked, so I'm being nice to you. Don't even think about what I'll do to you for arresting me."

"It was my job."

"This is mine, sweetie. This is what being with a Shareem is. He finds out all your desires and makes you live them."

"You can't know what I want," Deanna said.

"Bet me. I know you like this." Justin raised his hand and slapped it down on her backside again. "You like me spanking you."

"No."

"Then why are you letting me do it?"

"Because you've handcuffed me!"

"Deanna, love, those cuffs aren't that strong. I'm not level three. You're not struggling to get away. That tells me you like it."

Deanna *did* like it. She'd never admit it out loud, but the heat on her buttocks, his hand resting there, excited her amazingly. Even more when he lifted his hand away, and she clenched her body in anticipation.

What she felt next was not his hand, but his tongue, seaming between her buttocks and touching her opening. She jumped.

"You like that too," Justin said in his dark voice. "My naughty patroller." He lifted his beautiful tongue away, and *slap, slap,* his hand came down again.

Deanna pulled at her bonds, but he was right, she didn't try very hard. "Let me go."

"I don't think so. Now, what else did you do to me? Oh, yeah."

Justin reached to his box next to the bed and took out a plug that looked much like the one she'd used on him. Deanna caught the whiff of sanitizer when he removed it from its case then the sweet smell of lube.

"Wait," she said. "I don't think I'm ready for that."

Justin leaned down until his face was close to hers. She liked him so close, his sandpaper whiskers beckoning her touch. "You are ready, Deanna. You really are."

He held the plug where she could see it, while his big fingers deftly coated it with lube. He touched the plug to her lips. "Kiss it for luck."

She should arrest him. Deanna should rip open her bonds, jump from this bed, and arrest him for making her so excited.

Gingerly, she kissed the tip of the plug.

"Nice."

Justin slid his hand between her buttocks and gently rubbed her. He kept on rubbing, touching his fingertip to her opening, which Deanna felt widening and relaxing whether she told it to or not.

"There you go, sweetheart," Justin said in a low voice. "The plug is smaller than my finger. It won't hurt."

Deanna had no idea whether to believe him. The warmth of his fingertip went away to be replaced by the much cooler and stiffer tip of the plug.

She tightened, but Justin shushed her, heating her skin with his breath. When he touched with the tip again, Deanna unclenched her hands, forcing herself to relax.

"That's it." Justin pushed the plug a little bit inside her. "Now, we'll see. You'll either love it, or you won't."

The small thing felt strange inside her, where she'd never thought to put anything before. Justin didn't thrust it in or wriggle it but held it and let her get used to it.

Deanna closed her eyes, opened her body, and suddenly, the small plug went all the way inside. "Oh." She gasped. "Now I understand why you like this."

"You see? I didn't even push it in. You did that yourself." He leaned down to her. "Now, do you love it? Or hate it?"

"I love it." The babbled words came out of her mouth before she could stop them. "Justin, I love it."

"Good. We'll do more then, when you're ready. I'll teach you to take bigger ones, and then me."

"Yes. *Yes.*"

Justin had once told her that the plug would make her feel full and needy. And it did. It fulfilled her and at the same time made her want more.

Justin lay down next to her and slid his arm underneath her. "Come on over on top of me. I'll make you feel doubly good."

Before she could ask how, Justin pulled her thigh over him and positioned her against his already hard-again cock. He eased her all the way upright, the plug never moving, until he fit smoothly against her very wet pussy.

And then he was inside. Long and hard, pressing high into her as she straddled him, while the little plug filled her from behind.

The orgasm topped everything she'd had with him until now. Deanna came apart, twisting on him, every coherent thought gone, except her need to pull him *deeper*.

Justin, I love you!

She'd cried out the words before, now she whispered them in her mind. To herself, to keep them a part of her.

Darkness rippled through her, her only point of consciousness Justin and his hardness inside her, and the brilliant blue of his eyes. She let herself drown.

* * * * *

Justin came out of a pit of sleep to find his com beeping next to his head. Deanna was next to him, her head on his pillow, one leg over his.

Justin didn't want to answer the com, but it kept *beeping*. If he didn't shut it off, it would wake her.

He reached over and tapped its button. "What?"

"Is something wrong with your console?" came the voice of Elisa n'Arell. "I can't see you. There's only audio."

"You ask that, in a Shareem house? What is it? Did you find something?"

"Of course I did. Talan and me and Brianne." He heard the smile fill Elisa's voice. "We found her, Justin."

Chapter Sixteen

Of course, it couldn't be that simple.

"She's in the Way of the Sun, the most secluded of the orders," Elisa said. "I managed to get permission to go to the house, but only because Brianne d'Aroth still has a lot of power. I can go, and Talan, and though they said you could travel out there with us, Justin, there's no guarantee they'll let you set foot on the grounds or even talk to Lillian."

Deanna was up on her elbow, wide awake. "It's worth a try," she whispered.

"Yeah, thanks, Elisa. I really appreciate this. Let's see what happens."

"Does that mean yes?"

"It means, I'll be at Braden's in a few, and we'll discuss it." Justin cleared his throat again, trying to get hold of his emotions. "It means, you're a peach, and I owe you big time."

"We haven't seen her yet," Elisa said. "This might be all for nothing."

"You've still done a lot, Elisa. I'll be there."

Justin snapped off the com and lay down again, to find Deanna staring at him. "What?" he asked irritably.

"You should be jumping up, rushing off to see her. Happy for the chance, any chance."

"I am happy. I was worried as hell about her. I'm glad she's all right."

"But . . ."

"No buts. It's just . . ." Justin rubbed his hand over his face and found it bristly with new beard. "When all doors are closed, and suddenly they open, it's hard to get used to." He brushed his hand across her bare hip. The room was the perfect temperature, because the cooler had finally kicked in, but he wanted to curl up around the warmth of her. "Will you come with me?"

The words came out more wistfully than he intended them to.

"Of course," Deanna said. "I'm a patroller. I have the authority to make them let you see her if the situation is dire enough."

Justin looked into her eyes and found her looking back at him with openness and determination. She wanted to do this for him. For *him*.

For a Shareem who'd fucked up her life.

I love you, Justin.

She was tearing him apart.

* * * * *

Deanna watched Justin all the way out to the mountains the next morning, where the meditation center for the Way of the Sun lay, and wondered what was wrong with him.

They rode in a private car on a hovertrain, courtesy of Talan d'Urvey. The car was the ultimate in luxury and privacy, with a living room, bedroom, bathroom, and small kitchen in which servants could prepare the traveler any meal she wanted.

The car was also crowded, because it was meant for one very privileged woman, not four women and their Shareem.

Elisa, Talan d'Urvey, and Brianne d'Aroth accompanied Justin, and they each were followed by a possessive and watchful Shareem—in Brianne's case, two of them.

Deanna had met only Justin, though she'd seen—and carded—Shareem during her patrols. Braden, black-haired and easy to laughter, was with Elisa. Brianne was with Aiden, who immediately took possession of the sofa, and Ky, who kept quiet and made it clear he didn't trust patrollers. Deanna remembered seeing Aiden and Ky in the open door of the bar the day Justin had given her the veil and taken her to his apartment.

The Shareem who unnerved her the most was Rees, a Shareem she'd never heard of, let alone seen. He was a little taller than the others and stayed near

Talan, the small redhead. Though he talked readily with everyone in the car, Deanna sensed that he kept himself a little distanced from all except Talan, who was never far from the circle of his arm.

Deanna studied the women as she sat on a loveseat slap against Justin—Elisa tapping her handheld with Braden's arm firmly across her shoulders, Talan basking in Rees's attention, and Brianne seemingly comfortable on Ky's lap with Aiden reaching out to lay his big hand on her thigh.

These ladies were highborn, and each had given up big houses, cushy jobs, and social standing to be with their Shareem. They were still rich, still with some power because of who their families were, but they were no longer accepted in the circles of higher society.

And looking at them, they had no regrets.

"You know," Aiden said from the couch, where he lay supine. "One train car, five Shareem, four pretty ladies . . . anyone else thinking orgy?"

Braden chuckled. "How do you put up with him, Bree?"

"She has sex with me," Aiden answered. "Calms me down, every time."

"One of the ladies here is a patroller," Ky growled.

The rest of them went quiet, no noise but the rush of the train as they rocketed across glaring desert.

When Justin and Deanna had arrived at the station, Justin had openly held her hand, daring with his gaze for the others to say anything. Elisa had welcomed Deanna without hesitation, and the other ladies had followed Elisa's lead.

"She's *my* patroller," Justin said, putting his arm protectively around Deanna. "I'm the only one she gets to cuff. And don't think she hasn't."

His bantering tone made Braden laugh and Aiden smile, but Ky didn't soften. "Yeah, when she arrested you. Was it that exciting?"

"Actually, it was," Justin said. He covered her hand with his free one, squeezing it a little, reassuring her. "She had me down on the ground, with her hot ankles right in front of my face, making me want to lick all the way up her legs. Good times, friends."

"Level twos," Braden said, shaking his head. "They think bondage is one big joke. They make crappy Doms."

"Bet me," Justin said. "We just know how to play. We'll take *any* situation and make it better."

"Like a patroller arresting you for minding your own business," Ky said. He was angry, radiated it.

"She arrested me for going where I wasn't supposed to," Justin said. "She was doing her job."

"And for that, you want to go down on her?"

"Sounds good to me," Aiden said.

"Shut up, Aiden," Ky growled.

"Deanna's with me," Justin said, cutting through their words. "We're together, we're having sex like I've never had before, and she looks hot in nothing but my handcuffs. And if she wants *me* in the cuffs once in a while, I don't have a problem."

Deanna's face went hot, and Elisa sent her a sympathetic smile. "You get used to it. It's their way of explaining to each other that they like us."

Justin pulled Deanna close. "And our way of saying *don't touch her, or I'll beat the crap out of you.*"

Deanna noted that Justin didn't look at Ky while he said this last—he looked at Rees, who hadn't joined the argument at all.

Rees and Justin shared a long look, and Rees gave a nod. "She's with him," he said.

The other Shareem went quiet a moment, then shrugged and went back to paying attention to their ladies. As though Rees's word was final, the discussion ceased.

Deanna longed to ask why Rees's declaration silenced them all. And who Rees *was.* She'd never seen him in the databases, not that she'd looked specifically, but she'd have remembered coming across a Shareem like him.

But there was no privacy here, nowhere she could whisper questions to Justin without Rees overhearing. Rees gave Justin a nod, then he gathered Talan to him and kissed her hair.

Justin had won something, but Deanna wasn't sure what.

* * * * *

The priestess in charge of the Way of the Sun's meditation house was elderly but smooth-faced, and quiet, but in the way a mountain was quiet. A mountain didn't move much or make much noise, but just try to shift it.

The priestess came through the gate in the large wall surrounding the Way's property and talked only to Elisa, ignoring Deanna and Justin standing with her. Sister Orianna, once known as Lillian Passan, was in deepest seclusion, the priestess said, and for her to have visitors was beyond thought.

"However," the elder said, never looking at Justin. "Sister Orianna has expressed a wish to speak briefly with this person from her past. I have granted her this wish, on condition that the male does not enter the grounds belonging to the Way. I have arranged a meeting in the retreat center in the town. You will wait for her there. If Sister Orianna changes her mind, you are to leave and not seek her again."

Deanna wanted to argue, but Elisa crossed her hands over her chest and bowed to the priestess. "Yes, elder. I have gratitude for your kindness."

The priestess nodded as though taking her due, then she turned around and walked back through the gate. The gate, a solid wooden door, slammed behind her, shutting them out.

"That's it?" Deanna asked hotly. "Go back to that wide spot in the desert they call a town and wait for her to *maybe* come out to see Justin?"

"The Ways are famous for being antisocial," Elisa said. "I should know. They teach unbinding the mind from emotions and living for pure intellect." She shrugged. "It works for some. I'm sorry, Justin."

"That's all right." Justin sounded more irritated than angry. "We'll wait. We've come this far."

"The fact that the elder spoke to us at all is a good sign," Elisa said.

She sounded hopeful, but Deanna couldn't conjure much optimism. As a patroller, she'd dealt with members of the Ways—some of them came to the city on business for their orders.

The Ways held themselves above all laws and social rules, and patrollers hated dealing with them. Patrollers were charged to protect their members specially, but the women of the orders thought they could stroll around anywhere they liked, including the most dangerous of the off-world docks, without worry, plus they assumed all traffic would stop for them and that all market vendors would give them their wares for free.

Maybe in ancient times, the world had bent over backwards to serve the women of the Ways, but times had changed. If not for patrollers, whose services were never acknowledged, the ladies would never live to see their meditation gardens again.

Justin was strangely silent as they entered the town's retreat center and settled in to wait in a small, shielded garden. He held Deanna's hand as they sat on a wooden bench under a golden-flowered tree, rubbing his thumb over her palm and fingers, not letting go as they waited.

Deanna squeezed his hand in return. *I'm here for you*, she wanted to say.

She was in love with a Shareem. How had her life become this insane?

"Elisa n' Arell?"

The light voice sounded across the garden room, and Justin jumped to his feet. He didn't drop Deanna's hand, though, and she scrambled up beside him.

"Sister Orianna?" Elisa asked.

The woman didn't answer. She was swathed from head to foot in robes, her face concealed by light-colored veils. The way the robes fit her, the way the fabric whispered, Deanna guessed that the robes had been tailored for her from the most luxurious silks known. Strange that these ladies wrapped themselves in opulence, but their beliefs forbade them to enjoy it.

Justin said, "Lillian?"

The woman drew a breath. "I used to be called Lillian." She hesitated a moment longer, then she lifted the veils from her face.

The lady inside was no longer the pretty working-class girl from the holopics, her face now lined by years of hard work. Her brown eyes were soft, however, as she fixed her gaze on Justin.

"Justin," she said, her voice barely a breath. "I couldn't believe it when they told me you wanted to see me. After all these years." She walked down the flagstone path to them, her robes rippling, until she stopped a foot from Justin. She looked up into his face but didn't try to reach for him. "It really is you. My dear, dear friend."

* * * * *

Justin looked into light brown eyes that he'd first seen regarding him in trepidation when he'd walked into the experiment lab at DNAmo. DNAmo hadn't always been clear about what the high-paying jobs for working-class girls actually were, until the worker was thrown in with her first Shareem.

He had reassured Lillian that first day, and they'd quickly become friends, and then more than friends. They'd had a daughter together. And now?

Now Lillian was hidden behind layers and layers of silk and a new name, while Deanna Surrell, a patroller in a drab coverall, had become Justin's lady-love. And Justin knew that the right things had happened.

He felt Deanna try to draw back, to give him privacy, but Justin gripped her hand, keeping her at his side.

"What happened to you?" Justin asked Lillian.

Lillian smiled the warm, deep smile he remembered. "Why did I become a celibate in a secluded Way? Don't worry, Justin. I'm not here because of anything that happened with you or because I gave my body for experiments at DNAmo. One thing I learned fast about Shareem — they have inflated egos."

Both Elisa and Deanna nodded, then all three women laughed.

Justin didn't smile. "Why are you here, then?"

"The world got too much for me, to tell the truth. Watching my father and mother die, when they could have been saved if we'd had more money, and having to give up my child to protect her . . . It all took the heart out of me." Lillian shook her head. "I suppose I could have left the planet, but I didn't want to be that far away from them. I can't see any of them, but at least I can know they're across the desert in Pas City, even if my father and mother are only remembered by a marker."

"It sure was damn hard to find you," Justin said.

Lillian raised her chin, the defiant look he remembered. "I didn't know you were looking, did I? You'd gotten free of Bor Narga. Why did you come back? Are you insane?"

Yes. "I came to tell you I found Sybellie. Our daughter."

Lillian stilled. "You've seen her?"

Justin reached for her hand. Screw the rules. They both needed this. "Yes," he said. "She's beautiful."

Lillian wrapped her work-hardened fingers around his. "She must be all grown up now."

"She's twenty-four. Goes to graduate school at the university."

For a moment, neither of them spoke. Tears spilled down Lillian's cheeks, and Justin's vision blurred. He was acutely aware of Deanna warm at his side, her presence giving him strength.

"It broke me to give her up, Justin," Lillian was saying. "I never wanted to."

Justin squeezed her hand. "I know why you did. You'd worked at DNAmo; you were a sex-worker. If anyone put together that a Shareem was the father . . ."

Lillian shot a nervous glance at Deanna, but Justin shook his head.

"Deanna knows. She'll keep the secret, and so will Elisa. They both were instrumental in helping me find you."

"And why *did* you find me? To tell me our daughter is beautiful and break my heart all over again?"

"I want to set up a meeting with her," Justin said. "You have the right to do that as her biological mother, now that she's of age, without revealing your identity if you don't want to. And if I can be there, without anyone knowing but her—Lillian, I can finally meet her, tell her . . ."

He stopped as Lillian began shaking her head. "I don't want to see her."

"Why not? I sure as hell do."

"Because giving her up was the hardest thing I ever did in my life," Lillian said in a hard voice. "I put it all behind me. I don't want to be reminded of what I was ever again."

"None of what you did was your fault. You gave up Sybellie to protect her."

Again, Lillian shook her head. "I took the job at DNAmo for the money. I helped people do experiments on you, for the gods' sakes. They told me you couldn't form an emotional connection with anyone, but when I found out you were developing feelings for me, I let myself believe it was all because of me. I'd broken through to you. I was arrogant, and I didn't bother to hide the fact that I was proud a Shareem wanted a real relationship with me." She drew a breath. "Then the wrong people found out, and you paid the price. So did Sybellie. Another reason I'm here is that my ignorance and arrogance have ruined three people's lives. Better that I'm in seclusion so I can't do that again."

Lillian dropped Justin's hand and stepped back, as though again severing herself from her former life.

"You were young, and their rules were asinine," Justin said.

"Doesn't matter. I was careless, and I hurt you, and her. Our daughter is still in danger of someone discovering you are her father, and if they learn it because I try to contact her and meet her . . ." She trailed off. "No, Justin. I won't be careless again. Not even for you."

Justin went silent, the emotions he wasn't supposed to have whirling through him so swiftly they left him numb. The one emotion he didn't feel was surprise.

"I think I knew you wouldn't want to see her," Justin said slowly. "If you had, you'd have been able to find a way before this."

"I took my vows and retreated for a reason, Justin. I don't like the real world. It was never good to me."

"And the Way of the Sun is?"

Lillian's smile returned, and with it came a serene look. "Yes."

Justin exhaled, a part of him that hadn't relaxed in a long time unclenching.

He reached for her hand again, tugged her to him, and kissed her forehead. "Be well, Lillian."

"You too, Justin. I'm sorry."

"Don't be. Thanks for seeing me. It . . . helped."

The visit had closed a door that had needed to be closed for a while. Now Justin could move on.

Giving him one final smile, Lillian withdrew her hand from his grasp and tugged her veils back over her face. She turned around and walked out of the garden room without saying good-bye to any of them.

Justin blew out his breath. "Thanks, Elisa. Deanna." He squeezed Deanna's hand, which he'd never released. He'd held her like a lifeline the whole time. "How about we go home?"

Deanna gave him an incredulous look. "Wait a minute," she said angrily. "That's *it*?"

Chapter Seventeen

Justin's blue gaze fixed on her, his face showing no emotion at all. "What else is there?"

"Justin, you searched for her for *months*, you came all this way, and she won't even help set up a meeting with Sybellie. And all you can say is *how about we go home?*"

Justin put warm hands on Deanna's shoulders. "It's done, love." He kissed her forehead. "Thank you."

Deanna looked past him at Elisa, who shook her head and shrugged.

Justin said nothing as they made their way out through the streets of the small town. Since it was a town under supervision of the Way, the streets had heat shielding and trees growing in stone tubs along the curbs. They walked in comfort to the train, where the others were waiting, but they walked in awkward silence.

Justin kept quiet all the way back to Pas City, but he sat close to Deanna and cradled her hand in his. The other Shareem and ladies were subdued, even Aiden not joking very much.

When they reached Pas City and its glaring end-of-day heat, and Deanna said good-bye to all, Justin finally came out of his stupor.

"Where are you going?" he asked in a sharp voice.

"I have things to take care of," Deanna said. "I'm sorry things didn't work out with Lillian."

Justin's eyes narrowed, but at least he wasn't wearing that dead look anymore. "I thought you were coming home with me. I want you there."

Deanna wanted to be there too, but she did have things to do that she could not do from Justin's bed — as pleasant as it might be to stay there.

"I'll see you later." She couldn't kiss Justin in a public train station without getting him arrested, but she sent him a look that she hoped he'd take as caressing.

Justin seized her wrist, holding their hands down so they'd be concealed by their sunblocking robes. He looked at her for a long time, his need pouring through his touch.

Finally, he released her, scowling, and let her walk away.

* * * * *

"Elisa told me what happened," Rees said, as the two of them entered Rees's apartment. "Did you get the closure you wanted?"

"Yes," Justin said.

Talan and the other two ladies had decided to go shopping. The other Shareem had headed for Judith's bar, but Justin and Rees, by mutual agreement, had made their way to Rees's apartment alone.

Justin didn't like the churning emptiness that had hit him when he'd watched Deanna walk away from him at the train station. He never wanted to feel that again.

She'd been angry with him for not being more upset about the visit to Lillian. But once Justin had seen Lillian he hadn't been very surprised that Lillian wouldn't want to help him with Sybellie. Lillian had suffered and was working through her guilt. She'd chosen to retreat, while Justin still wanted to face things head on.

Justin also realized that he'd lost any desire to pull Lillian back into his life. Even if he hadn't met Deanna he knew he'd feel the same—what he'd shared with Lillian had been over long ago. Lillian had made a good life for herself, and Justin was happy to let her live it.

Rees dispensed an ale from his refrigerator and offered it to Justin. Justin drank, thirsty after the hot walk.

"I'm glad Lillian found a place where she's happy," Justin said. "She deserves it."

"So do you." Rees gave him a pointed look. "So do the rest of us. And now that your quest is over, are you ready to get us to Sirius?"

"No." The word jolted out of him. He could leave Lillian behind without worry, but there was the question of Sybellie, not to mention Deanna.

Pure, savage rage flashed in Rees's eyes, a raw emotion Justin had never seen in the man—or any man—before. The anger was so deep, emotion so primal that Justin regretted he didn't have Deanna's stun gun handy. He knew without doubt that right now, Rees wanted to kill him.

Rees swung away from Justin and stood still, fists clenched, back rigid, skin shining with sweat.

"You all right?" Justin asked after the silence had stretched. He kept his voice calm, as he'd learned to handling the more dangerous off-worlders on Sirius.

Rees turned around slowly. His eyes looked more normal, but he held himself carefully, as though only great force of will kept him from tearing the room apart.

"Sorry," he said. "You're looking at the results of a Shareem experiment by the top scientists of DNAmo. They wanted the ultimate Shareem, and they got a beast who can rip down walls." He smiled, but it was strained. "Talan knows how to keep me calm."

"Maybe you should call her, then, because you don't look calm, my friend."

"I'll be all right. I've learned how to handle it. Mostly. You were saying?"

"I hadn't said anything yet, but you're helping make my point. Let me ask you—would you race off Bor Narga and leave Talan behind forever?"

"You know damn well I wouldn't. But if you're saying you don't want to leave Deanna, bring her with you. By the looks of things, she wouldn't mind."

Justin shook his head. "I don't think she'd come. Her mother is ill—a radiation accident. Actually, that's what I wanted to talk to you about. I need to pry into some deep, dark secrets."

"I'm a walking deep, dark secret," Rees said. "Wait a sec." He took a long drink of ale and sank down on the bed built into the wall. "Okay. Fire."

Justin took a seat, held his ale glass loosely in his hands, and started talking.

* * * * *

Deanna's leave of absence ended the next day. She returned to her station, trying to ignore the curious stares of her fellow patrollers, to find out whether she'd be allowed to stay.

Her captain called her in for a major chewing out, which Deanna had expected, and which included instructions for her continued good behavior.

Sure thing, Deanna had thought while she'd mouthed, "Yes, ma'am." *No arresting people vouched for by the ruling family, no matter what they've done. Wouldn't want my captain to be embarrassed, or anything.*

And then she was back at work. They needed patrollers, her captain said, but Deanna was no longer on track for promotion. That would take another year of hard work, keeping her nose clean, and staying the hell away from Shareem.

The last part would be a problem, Deanna knew.

She also knew that Justin would not be able to keep himself from the Vistara. He hadn't seen Sybellie in two days, and he must be itching to go. Deanna had deliberately checked in early to get her reprimand out of the way so she could be sure to get up to the Vistara before Justin did.

When she walked into the coffeehouse on the wide avenue, Sybellie was alone. Not a coincidence, because Deanna had caused a few streets to be closed to keep the girl's friends from reaching the coffeehouse at their usual time.

"Oh, hello," Sybellie said. She smiled as Deanna stopped at Sybellie's table. "Thanks again for helping me the other day. Would you like me to get you a coffee?"

"No, thanks. But can I talk to you?"

"Sure. I'm waiting for some friends, but come and sit down. They're a little late, as a matter of fact."

"Probably stuck in traffic," Deanna said, taking the seat opposite her. "Some streets are closed. Leak of some kind."

"The streets were fine the way I come. I guess I got lucky." Sybellie took a sip of coffee and licked cream from her lip. "What do you want to talk to me about? The man who accosted me?"

"No. He's left the planet. I made sure. Are you all right about him?"

Sybellie grinned. "If you mean, do I have bad dreams and post traumatic stress disorder, then no. He was awful, but I'm pretty tough."

Like Justin. Sybellie had his eyes and his easy-going temperament.

"What I wanted to talk to you about was your father," Deanna said.

Sybellie looked confused, then alarmed. "Dad? He hasn't done anything wrong, has he? He's the most honest, law-abiding person I've ever met, I swear to you."

And she loved him. Deanna saw that in her face, heard the affection in her voice.

"Not your adopted father. I mean your real father."

Sybellie went still, brown eyes fixed on Deanna. The two sat in silence for a moment, and a waiter deferentially paused to refill Sybellie's cup.

When the waiter glided away, Sybellie spoke, her voice holding anger, though she stayed calm. "Anyone can find out I'm adopted by looking it up. But I'd like to know why you looked it up."

"What do you know about your biological father?"

Sybellie shook her head. "Nothing. I tried to find out who he was, once. I hired some very good researchers and paid them quite a lot, but they found nothing. Why? Is he a criminal? Or has something happened to him?"

"No, no," Deanna said quickly. "He's fine." She leaned to the young woman, keeping her voice down. "Would you like to meet him?"

"Meet him?" Sybellie asked in a stunned whisper. "You mean you know who he is?" She stared at Deanna another moment, then her eyes narrowed. "You aren't B.S.ing me, are you? Or scamming me or conning me? You're a patroller, but my dad's rich, and you're only human."

"It's not a scam or a con, Sybellie. I really do know who your dad is, and I really can take you to him. But you can't tell *anyone* about him, not your adopted parents, not your friends. No one. Not even that you met him. You have to swear to me your silence, or I can't take you at all."

"You're not instilling much confidence. Why is it such a secret?"

"I can't tell you, and you'll have to trust me. But I know he wants to see you. I can safely say it's the one thing in his life he truly wants."

"Is it?" Sybellie flushed. "Then where has he been the last twenty-four years? I've been *here*. Why hasn't he tried to see me before this?"

"He was off planet, and it took him a while to find you," Deanna said. "And then . . . Again, I can't tell you everything. But he needs you."

"Why? Why suddenly come to me now?"

"I'll let him tell you that, if he wants to." Deanna rose as the coffeehouse door opened, and Sybellie's friends came in, breathless from their brisk walk. Deanna passed Sybellie a tiny com device, pressing it under the girl's hand so the others wouldn't see.

"Take some time to think about it, then give me a call. But don't take too long, because he might be gone again."

Sybellie only stared at Deanna, but she was sensible enough to slide the com under her robes before her friends saw it.

The other young women approached, and Deanna turned away without a word.

"Hey, Syb," one of them said. "Sorry we're late. It's a mess out there. Why was that patroller talking to you? What did you do this time?" The three of them laughed.

"Oh, it was about that guy who was harassing me the other day," Sybellie said, giving them a sunny smile. "No big. I ordered for you all. Sit down—it should be ready any second."

* * * * *

Deanna spent the rest of her day wondering whether she should tell Justin what she'd done. How angry would he be? Or would he be glad Deanna had made the approach?

She'd certainly take precautions. The com she'd given Sybellie was secure, linked to Deanna's personal com and it alone. No patroller would break into it, because Deanna knew how to keep them out.

She also wouldn't tell Sybellie *anything* about Justin, until she was certain Sybellie wouldn't run straight to her adopted parents with the news. Deanna would control the information flow every step of the way.

Deanna finally went off duty, said good night to her colleagues—who'd decided that now she'd been let off probation, it wouldn't hurt them to talk to her again—and walked outside to good old Pas City.

Her feet wanted to take her to Justin's, but Deanna made herself turn instead for home.

As soon as she opened the front door, Deanna knew something was up. The air inside felt different, charged.

She saw why when she walked into the front room. Reda was sitting in the corner by the holographic window, staring not quite comfortably at the tableau on the sofa.

Deanna's mother reclined on the couch, a throw around her shoulders. She was watching, and actually listening, to Justin, who was seated beside her, Justin talking to Deanna's mother as though she could understand every word.

Chapter Eighteen

When Deanna entered the apartment, Justin felt his entire being relax.

I'm never letting her walk away from me again.

"Justin, what are you doing?" Deanna demanded.

She again wore her form-fitting coverall, her dark hair tamed into its severe bun. Back to being the tight-assed patroller.

"I'm talking to your mother," Justin said. "She was telling me about her accident."

Deanna glanced in surprise at Reda, who pressed her lips together and nodded. Deanna approached the sofa with careful steps, as someone might an injured animal.

"Mom?"

Kayla turned her head. The movement was slow and unpracticed, but she looked at Deanna fully. "Hello, Deanna. Back from work, are you?"

Tears flooded Deanna's eyes, and she put her fingers to her mouth.

"I was telling your friend what happened to me," Kayla said. She spoke slowly, the words not formed quite correctly, syllables slurred. "So he'd understand what a pain in the ass it is." She stopped, and her lips moved into a smile. "He's quite handsome, Deanna. Where is he from?"

"Sirius," Justin said before Deanna could speak.

Her mother looked him over, again her movements deliberate, as though she had to remember how to perform them. "I went to Sirius once, when I was younger. No one there looked like *you*."

"He's Shareem," Deanna said in a strangled voice.

Kayla looked puzzled, as though trying to remember the word, then her brow cleared. "*Deanna*. Bad, bad. No wonder he's hot."

Justin grinned. "So's your daughter."

"She lives for her work." Her mother sounded disapproving.

"Not if I can help it."

"Justin," Deanna said. "Can I talk to you?"

"And now she's mad at me." Justin winked at Kayla, took her hand gently between his, and squeezed it. "I'll be right back."

Her mother nodded. Justin rose to follow Deanna. As soon as they were across the room, her mother slumped slowly back against the cushions, closing her eyes.

Deanna took Justin to her bedroom. Yep, as he might guess, her private room was neater than neat. Her bed was tightly made, the room bare of everything but a bed, a small nightstand, a console, and a chair. He was surprised Deanna allowed the chair, but she likely didn't believe in sitting on the bed to work on her computer.

The crimson silk veil he'd bought her rested on her beside table.

Deanna shut the door behind them. She drew a long breath, but instead of shouting, or demanding, or scolding, Deanna flung herself at Justin and threw her arms around him.

Justin caught her to him, holding her close as she started to shudder.

As always, even touching Deanna in comfort aroused him. It had been too long—almost two whole days—since he'd had her. He kissed her hair, stroking her back, making soothing noises.

He wanted this. Forever. Not just sex with her, not just pleasure. But holding Deanna, comforting her, talking to her—being with her.

The rest of it didn't matter. Not Rees's plans, or the laws against Shareem, or the problem of leaving Bor Narga. As long as Justin could be with Deanna, none of it mattered.

Deanna's face was wet with tears. Justin brushed one away and kissed her.

Her mouth was warm. Deanna's lips answered his, her kiss as hungry as his own. When he pulled back, she sought him again, as though desperate to remain in the oblivion of the kiss.

"Deanna," he whispered. "It's all right."

"No, it's not all right," she said brokenly. "I'm happy whenever I see her like that—which doesn't happen very often anymore—but I know it won't last. The good days never do."

"She's not having a good day."

Deanna pulled back and wiped her eyes. "This is what a good day for her is. She looked at me. She knew me, knew I'd gone to work this morning. And she was talking to you —coherently."

"She wasn't when I got here." Justin released Deanna and reached for the hypo in the pocket of his tunic. "I gave her this."

Deanna stared at the hypo in surprise and then outrage. "And what the hell is that?"

"A concoction a doctor gave me. She asked me to tell her how it worked—the doctor, I mean. I think it's doing all right, but I also think my Shareem pheromones are boosting it."

"What concoction? What doctor? And why the hell didn't you tell me you were going to barge in here and *experiment* on my mother?"

Deanna knocked the hypo out of his hand, but the thing was made of tough plastic and only clattered on the floor.

"You weren't home," Justin said in reasonable tones. "It's working, Deanna. Once I tell my doctor friend, she can put together enough of it so that your mother can get to Ariel and the treatment center there."

"Treatment center." Deanna nearly spit the words. "On Ariel. The best in the known universe. Sure, I'd love to send her there, but *I can't afford* the treatment center on Ariel, let alone get her to Ariel. You know that."

"But I can."

She blinked. "What?"

"I made a lot of money on Sirius. I had my own offloading company, and it was very lucrative. The money from it is in accounts even Bor Narga can't stop me from accessing. My doctor friend said she might be able to treat your mother herself, but she's in hiding, and she thinks the Ariel facility will be more comfortable for her."

"In hiding? What do you mean she's in hiding?"

"Long story."

Dr. Laas, the brilliant researcher from DNAmo, who still had a price on her head for inventing the Shareem, had never left Bor Narga. She lived in an underground complex, hidden from the world, served by an annoying computer called Baine.

Dr. Laas was a genius. She'd saved Calder from certain death at DNAmo, when the other scientists had been ready to flush the plasma-burned Calder as a loss. She'd helped Ky when he'd recently suffered the aftereffects of an experiment, and she'd helped Rio and Nella hide out and get to Ariel. Dr. Laas wouldn't leave Bor Narga, she said, because the price on her head extended to every known galaxy. And besides, she'd add, she didn't want to leave all her Shareem.

Rees had agreed to contact Dr. Laas and tell her about Deanna's mother's problem. Katarina, Calder's lady, had gone to visit Dr. Laas, and the two of them had researched her case—Baine was good at hacking into records. They'd come up with this little hypo, which Katarina had given to Justin.

Apparently the concoction would help her mother's brain temporarily connect neurons or something. Katarina had explained it to Justin in medic-ese, until Justin had grabbed the hypo and said, "Whatever. I stick it against her neck and click. Got it."

"Justin." Deanna pressed her hands to her face. "This is crazy. I can't get her to Ariel. *You* can't even leave the planet . . ."

"But Katarina can, and Brianne and Talan can, and Rees has a couple of friends on Ariel—one happens to belong to the ruling family there. We'll wrap up your mom, stick her on a transport, and you and the ladies will take her the hell to Ariel. When she's better, you'll all come back." He forced a grin. "Unless you fall in love with the weirdness of Ariel and want to stay there."

"I won't if you're back here." Deanna snapped her mouth shut after the words, as though she'd not meant to say them.

Justin's heart flooded with hope. "Deanna, you're killing me."

"You're killing *me*. Why would you do this?"

"Because you need it."

They looked at each other, the room quiet, the red of the folded veil the only vivid color in it.

"I don't know what to do," Deanna murmured.

"It's simple. Take your mom, get on a transport to Ariel, and check her into the facility. While she's in treatment, go to a spa or shopping or whatever women like to do. I hear there's lots of that stuff on Ariel. Enjoy yourself."

Deanna shook her head. "I can't let you pay for it. I arrested you. If you pay for something for me, especially something as costly as a treatment center, for the gods' sakes, it will be viewed as corruption. I could be arrested, transported, or imprisoned. I shouldn't have even let you give me the veil."

Justin stared. "You are kidding me."

"Not kidding. The patrollers take corruption very seriously."

"This is your mother's life, Deanna."

"I know!" Her shout rang through the room. "I know that. Way more important than the rules of the damn patrollers."

She scrubbed hands through her hair, breaking the bond that held it back. Her hair tumbled down, loose and beautiful, the way Justin liked it.

"Please let me think about it," she said. "I have a lot to process right now."

"Think about it all you want. The offer stands for as long as you need it. I'm not going anywhere."

He wasn't. Helping Deanna, making sure she and Sybellie were all right, was more important to him right now than breaking free of Bor Narga. *One thing at a time.*

Justin went to her and gathered her to him, and they stood together for some time, holding each other, sharing comfort. Then Justin gave Deanna one last, lingering kiss, and left her alone.

* * * * *

Deanna sat with her mother for a long time after Justin left. The apartment seemed emptier without him. When she'd walked in tonight and seen him, she'd been struck by how well he'd filled up the room. Justin's big body had taken up half the sofa, his muscular arm stretched across its back, his long legs extended, Justin relaxed and comfortable.

So masculine against the fragile femininity in the apartment, and yet, he *fit* there. Her mother and Reda had watched him in surprise, not fear. He was a lion amidst lionesses and cubs, protecting, not threatening.

And now the apartment wanted him back.

Kayla remained mostly coherent and talkative for the rest of the evening, wanting to know all about Justin. Where had Deanna met him? What was their relationship? Why had Deanna been keeping him a secret? Unkind of her daughter, to not share she'd become friends with such a beautiful man.

Her mother seemed almost normal, except for her slow movements and her struggle to keep her speech from slurring.

As the night wore on, though, the drug wore off, and her mother relapsed to silence, but not an exhausted one. Kayla decided, of her own accord, to go to bed, where she fell quickly into a peaceful sleep.

There was no way Deanna could deny her mother treatment that would bring her back to her old self. No matter what the cost.

Deanna believed Justin when he said he could pay for it. He still owned the house on Sirius, and she knew that businesses on Sirius could be prosperous. Siriuns believed in hard work and lots of it, and were perfectly happy to reap the rewards of that work.

As a patroller, Deanna had been trained to be suspicious of even the most helpful person—what did they hope to gain? But she could only sit still and be grateful to Justin. He was a Shareem—a factory-made pleasure slave supposedly existing to sate his clients.

To Deanna, he was a warmhearted man who loved his daughter and was generous to his friends.

She loved him.

Deanna knew what she had to do—all of it. The choices were tough, but she knew that when made for the right reasons, they'd be the easiest choices in the universe.

But though she went to bed resolved, Deanna was uneasy about one thing. Sybellie had never called.

Chapter Nineteen

Justin stumbled awake the next morning to answer his door that was insistently chiming. If Braden was behind it, up early and chipper, Justin would have to kill him.

The door shot open to reveal Deanna silhouetted against hot Bor Nargan sunlight. "Hello, Justin."

Much better than one of his annoying friends, but she was definitely chipper.

"Can I come in?" she asked.

Justin blinked, rubbed one eye with the heel of his hand, and moved aside. "You're being polite? Not barging in using your patroller codes? Not that it was ever a bad thing for me."

"I don't have the override key anymore." Deanna walked inside past him and waited for the door to close behind her. "I turned it in, along with my stun gun and my badge."

Justin removed his hand from his eye to look at her fully. Deanna smiled back at him, appearing perfectly sane. She wore a black, kind of loose bodysuit today, her hair up as usual.

No, not as usual. Instead of the severe bun she always wore, she'd braided her hair and wound it into a coil. The style was soft, more feminine. She'd also knotted the red veil he'd bought her around her neck like a scarf to accent the black coverall.

Justin found his voice. "You look hot."

She went pink. "You look asleep."

"I *am* asleep. I dreamed you walked in here and said you turned in your stun gun and badge."

"I did say that. I resigned." She looked happy she'd just quit the job she'd once confessed was her entire life's purpose. "As I am no longer a patroller, I can take my mother to Ariel without conflict of interest. My captain assured me that this was true, when I told her what I wanted to do and why."

Justin's eyes widened. "What *exactly* did you tell her?"

"Nothing about you or your private accounts. I said a friend was helping me pay for my mother's treatment, and that I was quitting first so I wouldn't be accused of corruption. She agreed it was the best thing to do."

Justin's mouth was dry. "But what are you going to do? You want to be a patroller. You love arresting people, and stunning them, and cuffing them. It's your life."

"Very funny. The people I love are more important than my career. I can always start another career. I'll set up my own bodyguard service, maybe, or an investigation company." Deanna let out her breath. "You handed me something I desperately needed, Justin. It was a no-brainer."

Her face glowed, and her mouth wouldn't stop smiling. She was relaxed, for the first time since Justin had met her, not tense about anything. She'd made her decision, and it had given her wings.

"You're an amazing woman, Deanna Surrell."

"Not so amazing. I also did something that might make you angry." She bit her lip.

Did she know how sexy she was when she did that? "What did you do, Ex-patroller?"

"I told Sybellie I knew where her real father was and that I'd take her to meet him. If she wanted. I gave her my number." Deanna nibbled her lip again. "She hasn't called back."

Something cold and sharp cut through Justin's body. "You . . . told her."

"She deserves to know."

"*What* did you tell her?"

"Nothing specific, not even your name. Only that I could arrange a meeting with you. I'm not sure she believed me."

The world tilted under Justin's feet. "Deanna if she goes to her adopted mother or some higher-up patroller, even with what you've already told her, you could be hauled in and questioned until you spill what you know. And that will be it for Sybellie."

Deanna shook her head. "I think she'll wait until she has all the facts before she decides what to do. Sybellie struck me as having a lot of sense."

"That doesn't mean she trusts you. Why should she?"

Deanna gave him a patient look. "If Sybellie were the kind of young woman who ran to mama about everything, I'd have been hauled in within the hour. And even if I am questioned, I know how to keep my mouth shut. I won't betray you, or her."

"How are you going to do that? I know about the patrollers. They have drugs, they have coercion techniques . . ."

"Which I have the training to resist. If I thought I'd be putting Sybellie in danger, I wouldn't have approached her at all."

"Damn it, Deanna."

"What are you afraid of? That she'll be found out, or that you'll get to meet her? As her father I mean, not as the tongue-tied passenger in my car."

Justin folded his arms, the chill not leaving him.

The thought of Sybellie being harmed kept him awake at night. He needed to protect her at all costs.

But the thought of facing her and finding out what she'd think of having him as a father, made his blood ice cold.

At the same time, the possibility of getting to see her made Justin want to whirl in the middle of the room and laugh.

"Why the hell are you mucking around in my life?" he asked softly. "Making me crazy?"

"Why are you mucking around in mine?"

Easy answer. Justin cupped her shoulders, rubbing thumbs along her collarbone through the coverall. "I can't stay away from you, that's why," he said. "I need you to be all right."

"I need you to be all right too."

Justin let his touch turn caressing. "I guess we're stuck with it then."

Deanna moved closer, rising on her tiptoes, eyes half-closing. "Guess so."

Justin leaned to meet her, completing the kiss.

He relaxed into it, her lips sweet and pillow-soft. They hadn't done this very much—simple kissing. There'd been so much heat between them.

His heart beat faster when Deanna broke the kiss and licked his throat. Apparently she wanted more of the heat. Justin closed his eyes and let her seek it, enjoying the sensation of her lips and tongue on his skin.

Deanna didn't stop at that. She stooped and pressed a kiss to his chest, finding his male nipple through his tunic. She teased the nipple to a point with her teeth, while Justin's cock joined the rest of his body in becoming hard and tight.

She took her kisses down his abdomen to his navel beneath the tight fabric, then she sank to her knees and lifted the thigh-length tunic to expose his cock, dark and hard. Justin had pulled the tunic over his naked limbs to answer the door, so now there was nothing between him and the world, or Deanna's mouth.

She kissed the tip of his cock. Justin jerked, the breath going out of him. He searched for breath again when Deanna parted her lips and took his cock into her mouth.

His dreams were coming true. Deanna looked up at him, her brown eyes soft, her red lips wrapped around him.

Justin clenched his hands, slowing the thrust he wanted to take. She wasn't used to this. He needed to be gentle.

He'd taught her well, though. She started to suckle, pulling hard enough to make him tight with need, but not so hard to have him coming too soon. She tapping the underside of his cock with her tongue, teeth scraping softly, fingers coming up to stroke his balls.

Justin forced himself to stand still and take it. The front room was hot, his cooler still not working right. Outside the door, street traffic creaked by, the apartment not soundproof.

In the quiet warmth inside, Deanna's tongue danced and flickered over his cock, her mouth making little wet noises. The only other sounds were the swallowed groans in Justin's throat.

Justin dragged one hand through her hair, breaking the tie that held her braid, which fell like a silken rope into his palm. He opened his fingers and unwove the braid, holding her hair while she went on sucking him.

Her touch moved to his ass, she remembering how to warm him and open him.

Dear gods he loved this woman.

"I'm going to come, sweet lady," he said, his voice barely working. "And I want you to swallow me down."

Her gaze flicked up to him, her brown eyes steady.

"You don't have to," he whispered.

Deanna closed her eyes again. She moved both hands to his ass and held on tight.

Justin threw back his head, jerked his hips, and spilled his seed into her mouth. One jolt, then two, then mad spasms as he thrust, and thrust again.

His hand was in her hair, her sweet fingers on his ass, while Justin rocked his hips, coming inside her mouth until he'd given all he could give.

Deanna eased back on her heels, wiped the last drops of his come from her lips, and smiled at him.

I love you! Justin screamed inside his head. *Gods, how much I love you.*

He sank to his knees and gathered her into his arms, while he loosened her coverall to show her just how much.

* * * * *

One of the hardest things Justin ever did was say good-bye to Deanna before she and Katarina left with Deanna's mother and Reda for the transport to Ariel.

He and Calder said their farewells to them inside Deanna's apartment, knowing that Shareem wouldn't be allowed near the passenger dock at the Ariel liner. While Reda watched, rather disapprovingly, Justin pulled Deanna into his arms and kissed her, long and lovingly.

Again Deanna's mother seemed to perk up with Justin around. Katarina had continued giving her the doses of her concoction—whatever it was—in the week prior to the trip. Katarina theorized that Shareem pheromones had a calming effect on the nerves, which enhanced the reaction to the drug.

It worked. That was all Justin needed to know.

Deanna's arms tightened around him in one last hug, and she whispered, "Thank you, Justin."

She pulled away, but Justin kept hold of her hand as they left the apartment building, not releasing it until she climbed into the hovercar that would take them to the passenger docks. She couldn't kiss him out here, but her smile was nearly as good as.

Calder was having the same difficulty letting go of Katarina. His face wore a hard scowl as she finally peeled his fingers from hers so the driver could close the door.

The hovercar shot off, raising a cloud of dust that settled back over Justin and Calder. Calder coughed.

"If they decide to stay on Ariel," Calder said. "I'll kill you."

"Katarina's coming back," Justin said. "She's so madly in love with you it's sickening."

Calder didn't look convinced. But then, Calder had been horribly burned at DNAmo, even now bearing lingering scars of it, and he couldn't believe his luck at winning Katarina's heart. While still disfigured, he'd run a pleasure dungeon for ladies who wanted to be with the scarred "Beast," until Katarina had come into his life and saved him.

Calder turned and started walking away, the taciturn man rarely telling anyone what he was doing, or thinking . . . or anything.

"Where are you off to?" Justin said, falling into step with him.

"To get drunk. That's the only thing that's going to take my mind off being without Katarina."

"Shareem don't stay drunk long. You're going to have to try pretty hard."

"Who says I won't?" Calder shot him a dark look. "I'm going to be so damn horny, my hand will get blisters. I'm not like you. I don't get off on watching."

"I'm not really interested in watching anyone else anymore," Justin said. "But that reminds me of something I wanted to ask you. You still have that warehouse, don't you? With the dungeon hidden inside?"

"It burned," Calder said tersely. Hence a few of the newer scars.

"I heard from a reliable source—Katarina, in fact—that it didn't burn completely. She says that you and she have fixed it up again. I want to borrow it. I have a surprise in mind for Deanna when she comes home."

"*If* they come home."

"Katarina's coming back, asshole. Think of this time as an opportunity to figure out ways to show her how much you missed her."

Calder didn't exactly do a dance in the street, but his scowl lessened as he thought about that.

Justin laughed. "There you go. Now let's go fix up your dungeon."

They walked away, Justin's heart heavy, despite his laughter. He had far more reason than Calder to believe his lady might prefer to remain on Ariel. She no longer had a job here, and her mother would be well and happy . . .

And in the seven days between the time that Katarina had arranged a place at the treatment center and berths on the liner to get there, Sybellie had never once tried to contact Deanna.

* * * * *

By the second week of Deanna's departure, Justin was pretty much insane. Deanna contacted him every day to report her mother's progress, which was all good. The center anticipated a full recovery.

The tears in Deanna's eyes when she said it made their separation worth it.

Almost. Justin also enjoyed the new game he'd invented for them—he'd instruct Deanna on ways in which to pleasure herself, and Deanna would do it in front of the console in her bedroom.

One evening when they talked, Deanna said, "I'm wearing them."

"Yeah? Wearing what?"

"The balls. I put two in this morning before I went shopping with Katarina."

Justin's blood went hot, and he felt his eyes start to change. "And you've been walking around with them inside your pussy?"

"Yes." Her color rose.

"How do they feel?"

"Good." Deanna smiled, her breath coming faster. "Whenever I think of you, it's even better."

"You're a sweetie." His hand went to his leggings, untying them so he could dip inside and soothe his already tingling cock.

"Justin." Deanna ran her tongue around her lips, and his cock took another leap. "I want you to do something for me."

"Name it, baby."

"Instead of you watching me do something, I want to watch you."

His heartbeat sped up. "Fine by me, Angel. What?"

She told him.

* * * * *

It really wasn't fair she was so far from home, Deanna thought, as Justin darkened his screen to prepare. Or that Shareem weren't allowed to travel off planet.

The two little balls she'd lubed and worn inside herself, under the silken leggings she'd bought on Ariel had felt odd but satisfying. If she imagined Justin's fingers rubbing her at the same time, it made her nearly orgasmic.

When Justin brought his screen to life again, she thought the orgasms would commence.

He'd seated himself on a chair, naked, his torso gleaming with oil. He'd somehow wrapped ropes around his body, ending with cording them around his wrists.

He leaned back a little, the pleasing plane of his hard body one long line from ankles to chin. In the middle, his cock stood upright, unhindered by the ropes.

"Is this what you wanted?" he asked, his voice low.

Deanna could barely breathe. "Yes."

"Good." Justin leaned back a little more, chest moving as he adjusted the ropes. "Then command me."

Chapter Twenty

"Wait." Deanna tapped a button on her console to take a still shot of the beautiful Justin, tied up for her delectation. "Now, um . . . touch yourself. Like you tell me to touch myself. Make it exciting."

He shot her a look, and Deanna shivered in pleasure.

Justin had fixed the ropes so they'd be loose enough for movement while appearing to be tied. He placed his bound hands under his cock and ran his thumb up the underside. A small shudder went through him when he touched the sensitive place below the tip.

He reached down again and cupped his balls, then slid his closed hand up the cock. The tip grew dark red in the circle of his thumb and fingers, the head engorged with wanting.

"More," she said.

Justin moved his hands to his chest, brushing carefully over his skin, before he plucked one of his nipples between two fingers. When it was dark and tight, he moved to the other.

Once he'd brought that to a point, he reached into the box he'd placed at his side and took out something hidden by his hands.

A nipple clamp, she saw when he clipped it on to one of his hardened nipples. He groaned a little, letting her know he felt it.

Next came a cock ring, which he slipped easily on to his stiff cock, making the cock stand a little more upright. Finally, to another ripple of anticipation in Deanna, Justin lubed up a little butt plug, leveraged himself off the chair, and closed his eyes while he slid it inside.

He eased himself back down, rocking his feet up to his console desk and placing them on either side of the monitor. Deanna could see the plug between his parted legs, the ring, and his cock standing straight up.

His hands, still tied, stroked their way up his cock. The tip squeezed through his fingers, Justin breathing faster as he worked.

He was beautiful, a hard-bodied man lying before her with his legs spread, that huge cock pointed to the ceiling while he stroked it. Deanna remembered the taste of it on her tongue, wished she could lean forward and lick it from base to head.

Justin's fingers licked it for her. His broad fingertips rubbed from his balls upward, the tip jumping as he reacted to the pressure. The cock ring was strangely erotic, circling him at the base, making the shaft even darker.

"I wish you were with me, baby," he said. "This would be your hand on me, you stroking me off."

Yes, it would be. Deanna remembered when she'd rushed into his apartment to find him leaning against the wall, doing himself, how her blood had tingled, how she'd itched to touch him.

"I want you here sucking me," he said. "I want to see my cock going into your pretty little mouth, you closing your lips over me."

Without noticing she did it, Deanna lifted her first two fingers and slid them into her mouth.

Justin flushed. "Yeah, like that, sweetheart. Suck me now."

Deanna started to suckle, mouth working, her fingers wet, while Justin squeezed his cock in his fist.

"You're so beautiful with something big in your mouth," he said softly. "Did you know that, Deanna? You'd be even more beautiful if you played with your clit at the same time. Will you? Pretty please?"

Deanna removed her fingers from her mouth with a little popping sound. "I'm supposed to be commanding you."

"I know. I can't help it. Shareem like to control."

"No kidding."

Deanna had abandoned drab coveralls and sunblocking robes on mild Ariel, buying herself colorful silk tunics, leggings, and sheaths. They were wisps of almost nothing, and amazingly cheap. She and Katarina had gone a little crazy.

She untied the tunic and let it fall open to reveal her unfettered breasts then unfastened the leggings and let them drop. The brush of silk as it slid down her legs was sensuality itself.

"Oh, yeah," Justin whispered. "You'd better bring some of those home and wear them for me."

"I will."

He stilled his hand. "You are coming home, Deanna."

It wasn't a question, but she heard the uneasiness in his voice. "Of course, I am."

"If you don't, I'll have to spank your ass."

Her skin tingled, remembering his warm hand slapping down on her backside. "What about if I do?"

Justin smiled, slow and dark. "I'll spank you even harder. For right now, though, I want to watch you, while you watch me."

Deanna dipped her finger to her clit, bringing it back up to show him how it glistened with her need. Justin's eyes filled even more with blue as she raised her finger to her mouth and licked it clean.

His moan drifted through the speaker. "You are wonderful, Patroller."

Deanna slid her hand back down to her very wet pussy. With the balls still inside, her nipples as tight as could be, she rocked on her fingers, close to coming.

She feasted on the vision of Justin, thighs parted, cock huge, his eyes on her as he stroked himself.

Deanna rubbed herself faster in response. Justin did likewise, until they were both panting, making little noises of longing.

"Aw damn," Justin said, his bound hands moving swiftly. "I'm gonna blow, baby. Oh . . . *gods.*"

He kept pumping, his body moving on the chair, it creaking under his weight. A stream of white suddenly fountained up from his cock, falling back down over his hands, his balls, the cock itself.

Justin was right, watching was wonderful—as long as she was watching *him.* Deanna's pussy clenched over her fingers, ecstasy spiraling through her.

Everything went dark except the beautiful image on her monitor—her hot, naked Shareem, bringing himself off for her.

"Justin!" she said, then her cry of release rang across the stars.

* * * * *

"I miss you," she whispered a while later.

Deanna had removed the little balls and dropped them into her sterilizer. Justin was still bound, his hands unmoving now as he caught his breath, but the ring remained around the base of his cock. He grinned at her, eyes losing the wild blue, but he was still hot, still aroused.

"I miss you too, baby."

She liked this, smiling with him while they both calmed. Deanna wished she could be in the room with him, lying on his naked body and feeling him gather her close.

"But I'm glad I came," Deanna said, settling back into her chair. She didn't resume the tunic. Why should she? Her lover liked looking at her, and he made her feel that her body was beautiful. "My mom's so much better," she went on. "I can't tell you how grateful I am for you and Katarina, and what you've done. I'll pay you back . . ."

"Shh," Justin said. "No paying back. I'm glad I found a good thing to spend my money on."

She let her smile grow sinful. "I'll find some way to show you how grateful I am."

Justin laughed, brushing his hair from his eyes with his bound wrists. "I'm looking forward to it."

They were quiet again, never mind the astronomical cost of the planet-to-planet interface.

"I need to tell you," Deanna said softly after a time. "Sybellie still hasn't tried to get in touch with me. I'm sorry."

"That's all right. It doesn't matter."

Deanna knew it damn well *did* matter to him. "I'll try to contact her again."

"That might not do any good. She and her friends aren't meeting at that coffeehouse anymore. I don't know where she goes now."

Alarm flitted through her afterglow. "Justin, you aren't still going up to the Vistara, are you?"

Justin avoided her gaze. "Discreetly."

"You know that your pardon was only good for the one time. If you're arrested again, even Brianne might not be able to free you."

"I said *discreetly*, as in, no one sees me."

"Just don't. Please. Stop going. When I get back, we'll figure this whole thing out."

Justin didn't answer. Deanna seethed in frustration about the light years between them. She couldn't change his key codes and lock him into his house from the distance of Ariel.

Of course, she'd quit her patroller job, so she wouldn't be able to do it even on Bor Narga. But at least on Bor Narga she'd be able to stand next to him and yell at him.

"Justin."

"Yeah?" He looked up from whatever distracted place he'd gone to.

"Remember, when I told you I loved you?"

"Yeah." His worry left him, and his face softened with his smile. "I remember. Why? Want to take it back?"

"No," Deanna said. "I wanted to tell you, I meant it."

* * * * *

Discreetly, Justin had said. That meant he wore plenty of clothing and sunblocking robes and took a tinted-windowed car up to the Vistara. He had Elisa hire him a different one every day—Shareem couldn't hire cars themselves—so no one would report the same vehicle lingering on the streets.

Justin looked every day for Sybellie, but he never spotted her. Not at the coffeehouse, not on the campus, not in the shops around it. He knew where her house was, thanks to Elisa's information, but she must be staying with a friend, because she didn't go home. Or, Sybellie might have gone home when Justin was back in Pas City—Justin couldn't afford to stay too long each day.

Deanna was right, though. He needed to be careful. He had something to keep himself free for now.

And then, the day after he did his self-bondage session for Deanna, Justin found Sybellie.

His daughter walked along the street on the edge of the university's campus, a little pack at her side for her handheld and whatever other devices she carried. She was alone, her friends nowhere in sight.

Justin couldn't stand it. He turned off the car, unsealed the door, got out, and walked quickly to the campus.

He was covered from head to foot, sunblocking material over his nose and mouth. As soon as he stepped onto the campus, he felt the air cool, the protective shielding shutting out the worst of the sun's heat.

Sybellie strolled along, her head down, mind on wherever she was going. Justin stepped in front of her, and she stopped.

"Excuse me," she said politely.

She started around him, but Justin stepped in front of her again.

Now Sybellie looked up in alarm, mouth open to call for help. Justin unwrapped the material from his face and said, "Sybellie."

"Oh." She looked relieved but puzzled. "Mr. Justin, right? You're friends with that patroller."

"Yes."

He didn't move, and Sybellie frowned. "It's nice to see you Mr. Justin, but I have a class."

"Can you talk to me for just . . ." Justin swallowed, his voice not working. "Just a minute."

Please, please, just a minute to let me look at you.

"Did Deanna send you to persuade me to call her?" Sybellie asked. "Can you tell her I haven't made up my mind yet? I still have to think about it."

"No." Justin clenched his hands at his sides. "Deanna didn't send me."

"I shouldn't be talking to you about it then."

She turned slightly, and Justin stepped in front of her again.

"Sybellie." He loved the sound of her name. "Deanna didn't send me."

"You've just said that."

"She'll want to kick my ass when she finds out." Justin couldn't stop himself putting his hand on Sybellie's slim shoulder. "But I couldn't wait anymore. I had to see you."

Sybellie frowned, her mouth forming the *wh* of *Why?*

Then she stopped, her mouth going slack. She looked at him, *really* looked at him, and took a step back.

"It's you," she whispered. "It's you, isn't it?"

Justin could only nod, his throat closed too hard for him to speak.

"How can it be?" Sybellie asked. "Who *are* you? I don't even know your name. Your entire name, I mean."

Justin smiled a little. "It's just Justin."

"But . . ." Her eyes filled with sudden tears, and she shook her head. "This isn't fair. I have a class. But I have to talk to you, I have to ask you . . . *everything*."

Justin squeezed her shoulder, wishing he dared pull her close, but too many people walked across the busy campus. "I'll wait. I'll wait here for you, and we'll talk. I've been waiting twenty-five years."

"Oh, gods, this is so not what I thought it would be like." Sybellie wiped her eyes. "Damn it, I have a *class*."

Justin started to laugh, but his laughter was drowned by a sudden and sharp-pitched siren. Sybellie's eyes widened. "Sandstorm!"

So the nice people on the Vistara got a warning siren, did they? In Pas City, the wind simply howled through the streets, and the people dove for the nearest shelter.

Sybellie fumbled for her breath mask. "So much for class. And the shelter is all the way over there." She pointed down the artificial green of the campus.

"The campus is shielded, isn't it?" Justin looked up at the sky through the shield, where not even a stray speck of dust yet marred the blue.

"Against the sun. Not sandstorms. Crap, we won't make it."

Justin saw it now, a wall of dirt pouring down the wide avenues toward them. The far buildings on the campus were already engulfed.

"My car," he said. "Run!"

"Your car's shielded from sandstorms?"

Justin grabbed her hand and propelled her into the street. The heat and wind struck them with force as soon as they left the protected campus.

Justin unlocked the door and shoved her inside, sprinting around to the driver's side. Now to see if he could start up and get the hell out of there before the sandstorm flipped the car over and ground it to a pile of metal.

The doors sealed, shutting out the smell of dirt. *Warning,* the car's computer told him as soon as he brought it to life. *Approaching sandstorm.*

"No shit," Justin said.

Nearest shelter at seventeen degrees.

"Fine."

Justin hit the "Accept" button, which would let the car calculate wherever the hell seventeen degrees from their position was. The car obediently started to move, but too slowly for Justin's peace of mind. He'd just found his daughter and had dragged her into the path of a killer sandstorm . . .

She sat next to him, eyes wide as she watched the storm come, her hand gripping the handholds. Her breath came quickly, but she wasn't screaming in panic or screeching at him to do something. *She seems to have a lot of sense,* Deanna had said. He was so proud of that.

The shelter was a low building about a block away, whose doors started to slide back into concrete and steel walls when they reached it, again, too slowly for his comfort.

The sandstorm hit them. One moment, Justin was looking at the steel doors in white walls, the next, he couldn't see them at all.

"Fuck, fuck, fuck."

He hit the accelerator, screw waiting for the car to calmly drive itself into the shelter.

The car leapt forward, brushing the still-moving doors with a metallic shriek. A blast of sand-laden wind picked up the rear of the car and slammed it forward, spinning the car around.

Justin saw the dim interior of a small, single-car shelter whirling before them, then the sand pouring in at them, then the automated shelter doors as they met and closed.

The doors sealed. The sand that had blown in smashed itself against the car and the walls of the shelter, then dropped harmlessly to the ground.

Justin shut off the car and twisted to face Sybellie. "You all right?"

Sybellie pulled off her silk veils, flapping sand out of them. Her hair glistened in the car's weak interior light, brown streaked with gold.

"I'm fine. Just dirty. Do you always swear in front of women?"

Justin grinned. "Yeah. Yeah, I do."

Sybellie grabbed her handheld. "Let me tell my parents I'm okay."

"Sure."

Sybellie quickly typed a message, then tossed her handheld, her pack, and her veils into the back seat and let out a long breath.

"Well," she said. "I guess we have time to talk now."

Chapter Twenty-One

Justin's fingers shook as he set the car's internal air controls. "I guess we do."

"All right then. Who are you, who is my mother, why did you have me, why did you give me up, and why did it take twenty-four years for me to be able to ask you these questions?"

"Shit." Justin raised his hands. "Give me a sec."

"You've had twenty-four years."

"I know. It's complicated. What did Deanna tell you?"

"That you were off planet, that I couldn't tell anyone about you, not even my adopted parents. Tell me why."

She was going to make him spill everything. Not, *you're my dad, that's great, let's go for ice cream.* Sybellie wanted to know who he was. *What* he was.

Justin cleared his throat and decided to get it over with.

"I'm Shareem."

Sybellie's expression didn't change. "What's Shareem? What planet is that from?"

"A Shareem is from Bor Narga, and he's a man who looks like me." Justin's eyes narrowed. "And, by the way, if you ever see a Shareem who's *not* me, you stay away from him. Don't talk to him, don't smile at him, don't even let him know you noticed him. Promise me." If any of them touched his daughter, Justin would explain how much he didn't like that by cutting off the part that Shareem held dearest.

Sybellie fixed him with a steely look. "You still haven't told me what a Shareem is."

"You know, I'm glad you don't know." But Sybellie deserved the truth, and if she despised Justin for it, then she did. "Shareem were created in a factory. Made by a company called DNAmo, a long time ago. Most Bor Nargans don't think we're even human. But we are." Talan had once proved, by making a DNA examination, that they were.

"DNAmo." She looked thoughtful. "I've heard of them. Didn't they manufacture the perfect servants, or something? Then they were shut down."

"They were shut down because of Shareem. They did make the perfect servants—majordomos and butlers and maids—then they went on to creating slaves. Like me."

Sybellie's eyes widened. "You can't be a slave. Slavery's illegal."

"Was a slave. Or—I don't know if they ever managed to make us truly obedient. We're all pretty good at doing what we want." Justin curled his fingers into his palms. "We were pleasure slaves."

"Oh."

Was that an "Oh" of disgust? Surprise? Outrage?

Not something a man wanted to tell his daughter—*I was born and bred for fucking, to be the best at sexing women who paid DNAmo for the pleasure.*

"Sorry," he said.

"For what?" Sybellie's voice was quiet.

He risked a look at her. She was studying him, but with intense interest, not derision. "For not being a prince or something equally impressive. For having been created in a vat full of chemicals, for being a slave who ended up as a dock worker on another planet. And now I'm back here, where I'm the lowest of the low. I bet this is not what you always dreamed your father would be."

"I didn't dream about it much, to be honest. I was curious, yes, but I realized how lucky I was to be where I am, with parents who love me."

"Good," Justin said fervently. "I'm glad they do."

"And my real mother? Where is she?"

"Her name was Lillian. She was a girl from Pas City who signed on to be a guinea pig at DNAmo, to take part in experiments with Shareem. I won't tell you what kind of experiments, but you can probably guess. When she found out she would have you, she quit, and I was shipped off planet. Now she's a celibate in the Way of the Sun." He smiled shakily. "Your crazy parents."

"So you were never lifemates?"

Justin shook his head. "Never had the chance. They sent me off, and I never saw her again."

"And you're sure, one hundred percent sure, that the baby she had was me? And that you are the father?"

"If you want a DNA test, we can do that. I know a medic . . . she's off planet right now, but she'll be back soon. But even if you do take the test—you can't tell anyone. It's too dangerous. My medic friend is the only one we can trust to keep the results secret."

"I'd like the DNA test," Sybellie said. "But only so both of us can be certain." She reached over and put her hand on his arm. "But I believe you."

Relief flowed through him, and an elation that drove away every moment of despair and heartache of the last twenty and more years. He wished Deanna could be here to share the moment with him, but she'd be back. She'd be back, and Justin would never let her go again.

"Now tell me why it's too dangerous for anyone to know you're my real father," Sybellie said.

"Because Shareem aren't supposed to be dads. They created us to be sterile. Guess it didn't work, at least not on me."

"And so if people knew I was half Shareem . . ."

Justin's worry returned. "I have no idea what they'd do to you. Test you, sequester you, open you up and have a look inside. At best, they'd classify you as Shareem, and then no more graduate degree, no more nice house on the Vistara, no more friends. No more anything. I can't do that to you."

"You mean they'd say I wasn't human. Or not completely." Sybellie looked somber but not afraid. Deanna had said she was smart. "And on Bor Narga, non-humans don't have the same rights as humans."

"We are human," Justin said. "My friends have proved that—ladies of other Shareem. But the Bor Nargans won't admit it."

"Why not?"

"I don't know. I guess because Shareem represent a time before sexual inhibition, when things around here were a little crazy."

"We all study that in history. Bor Narga was once a barbarian culture, with women little better than slaves. But that was a long time ago. No one would want that again."

Justin shrugged. "Doesn't matter. I think people believe that if Shareem are allowed to run amok, society will degenerate back to barbarian times."

"Ridiculous."

"Try telling that to the ruling family. They like ruling. Anything they see as a threat to that, they stomp." Justin opened his hands. "That's the way it is."

"Not if I have anything to say about it."

"Sybellie, no," Justin said quickly. "Keep your mouth shut. You don't know about Shareem, you don't know I'm one, and you have nothing to do with me. I won't see you again. I just wanted to today. At least once."

She gave him another patient look. "I can help Shareem without revealing I am one. No one will know without checking my DNA against yours, right?"

"I think so. My medic friend knows all about that shit."

"Then I won't take the test, if it makes you feel better." Sybellie lifted her chin, a stubborn little tilt that made his heart burn.

"But you want to be sure," Justin said.

"Not if it endangers us. What if someone else saw the results?"

"Katarina would destroy the results before that could happen."

"It's still risky. If you've been looking for me all this time, have been following me around wanting to talk to me . . . then you must be sure."

"But . . ."

Sybellie shot him an exasperated look. "Now I know you're my dad. You're driving me crazy."

Justin started laughing. Happiness tore through him, and his heart broke.

He reached for her, elation filling him when she didn't shrink away.

He gathered her into his arms. Sybellie seemed shy at first, but then she put her arms around him, her body feather-light, and Justin had the joy, for the first time, of holding his daughter close.

* * * * *

Justin swore that the sandstorm was the shortest in Bor Nargan history. He and Sybellie spent it talking about everything—her life, her studies, her hopes and ambitions. He learned that she was very good at soccer and met her soccer companions every day after practice for a little snack before midmorning classes—the other three young ladies in the coffeehouse.

She wasn't as good at poetry and music, she confessed, but not bad at finance. Her mother liked that—her adopted mother—who half-owned a bank. Sybellie would probably end up working there, hence why she was going for a higher degree in techno-finance.

Justin let her rattle on, happy to sit back and listen to her. Sybellie asked about him, and he gave her a truncated version of his life on Sirius, but he quickly switched the topic back to her.

All too soon, the safe siren sounded and the shelter's doors slid back, revealing the street coated with sand, the sunshine as strong and clear as ever.

"I guess I'll have to go to class after all," Sybellie said. "They don't cancel for sandstorms—they just push back the schedule for the rest of the day."

Justin made no move to start the car and drive out. He feasted his gaze on his daughter's sun-streaked hair, her fresh, round face, her smile.

He couldn't let this be the last time he talked to her. He wanted to know more and more, to talk away the empty years.

"Sybellie, when—"

Sybellie gasped, her face paling as she looked at something behind him. Justin jumped around to see five patrollers in front of the car, pointing guns at him.

What the fuck? Justin popped the door to ask the question.

Five stun pistols trained on his face, and two pairs of hands hauled him out of the car. He found himself shoved face-first against its side, a stun gun digging into his ribs.

"What, sheltering from sandstorms is illegal now?" he ground out against the car.

"What are you doing?" Sybellie cried, having climbed out the other side.

The patrollers ignored her, which made Justin relax a little. They hadn't come for her.

"Three witnesses watched you abduct this woman," one of the patrollers said. "And I know we've had trouble with you before. You're finished, Shareem."

Cuffs bit into Justin's wrists, but he clamped his mouth shut. Let them think what they wanted, let no one mention Sybellie's name.

But Sybellie wasn't a girl who sat quietly with folded hands. "What are you doing?" she repeated. "He was *helping* me."

"He's a Shareem, and a nuisance, ma'am," a patroller said.

"He got me to safety. You leave him alone."

"If he brought you in here, it wasn't for safety. Did he touch you, ma'am? If so I can terminate him right here."

"*Terminate* him?"

"It's the death penalty for a Shareem to touch a woman without permission," the patroller said. She was a big, muscular woman, with none of Deanna's softness. "This one's already wanted for violating restrictions. You can file your report against him down at the station, or from home. It's up to you."

"File my report . . ."

Justin lifted his head and glared at Sybellie. "Get out of here. Go. Get away from me — "

The patrollers banged his face into the car. Justin grunted, tasting blood.

"Stop that!" Sybellie shouted. "Do you know who my mother is?"

They didn't care. Patrollers were ruled by the whims of the rich, but not when they were arresting someone who so obviously — to them — deserved to be arrested.

"Get the hell out of here!" Justin yelled at her. She couldn't let her name be associated with his, not for a second.

He heard the thrum of stun guns, then heat sliced through his side. As blackness swam at him, he heard his own voice still begging Sybellie to go. He saw her reach for him, and he smiled at her, his daughter, so beautiful.

"Good-bye," he said softly before he felt the bite of a second stun burst.

* * * * *

Deanna gazed through the thick plasti-glass of the cell at Justin, who was sprawled facedown on the floor. They'd taken his clothes, and only a thin cloth around his waist protected his privates. It had fallen forward as he lay, baring his firm, smooth ass.

"Oh, Justin."

Deanna put her hand on the glass, as she'd done when she'd first seen him in a cell, when he'd regarded her with Shareem-blue eyes full of anger.

He'd been worried sick that she'd find out about his daughter. She understood that now. From the look of things, he'd been worried sick about Sybellie this time too, which was why they'd kicked and stunned him.

"I can't believe you're vouching for him, Deanna."

One of the arresting patrollers, a large woman called Vrina, stopped outside the cell, folding her muscular arms.

Deanna and Vrina had never had any conflict, but they'd never been friends, either. Vrina liked to walk around the docks harassing off-worlders in her spare time, while Deanna preferred to go home and read books to her mother.

Deanna shrugged, not explaining. Keeping Justin from termination had been tricky, and had needed Deanna's official word that the Shareem worked exclusively for her now, with a backup statement from Brianne verifying this.

Katarina, the medic, told the patrollers that she'd shot Justin full of so many neutralizing drugs—at

Deanna's request—that he couldn't possibly have gotten his cock up to do anything to the young woman in the car. Katarina had even provided documentation.

The three women were careful to not mention Sybellie's name, and Deanna had forbidden her to come down to the patrol station.

Deanna had wanted to kiss Katarina and Brianne. Katarina had dummied up documents on the fly, and Brianne had serenely explained to the judge that she'd sent Justin to the Vistara on an errand, thinking that since Justin had been released last time at her request, she had the right to do that.

Justin had been granted a stay of execution, but for the last time, the judge had said severely to the three women. "Keep your pet Shareem at home where he belongs," she'd finished and thrown them out of the courtroom in disgust.

Vrina looked at Justin on the floor and shrugged. "I don't know what you see in him. He's too hefty. I like my men to be smaller than me."

So she could bully them, she meant. Deanna kept herself from rolling her eyes and said, "I like him the way he is."

"Whatever." Vrina pushed some buttons on her handheld. "Take him out of here. If someone finds him on the Vistara again, though, he'll be terminated on sight."

A square in the cell wall slid back, and Deanna walked in and fell to her knees beside Justin.

Justin woke from a wonderful dream of being wrapped around Deanna to find her here, next to him, her pheromones touching him. He was on the floor, mostly naked, and she had her arms around him.

Nice.

He jumped all the way awake, and groaned. Waking brought pain.

"Deanna? What the fuck are you doing here?"

"It's nice to see you too. I came back when Brianne sent word you were in trouble again. Now I'm taking you home."

"Shit."

"You can stay in here if you want," she said.

"Bite me." Justin couldn't help grinning at her, despite his fears. "But in a good place." She looked beautiful in whatever complicated silk garment she was wearing, her lovely face framed by gauzy veils.

"Shut up, Justin. Can you walk?"

"Out of this place? I damn well can."

He had to lean on her, though, as Deanna took him out through the door and down the cell block.

They'd confiscated his clothes, but Deanna had brought a tunic and sunblocking robe for him, sweet thing. He pulled them on, groaning at his sore muscles, but sore muscles would be a small price to pay. He was leaving the detention block with Deanna, instead of being marched to the termination chamber.

Not until they were checked out of the facility and back on the scalding street did Justin voice his worry.

"Sybellie?" he asked softly.

"Is fine." Deanna squeezed his arm. "You idiot. We kept her out of it, but she wants to see you."

"Where is she?" Justin asked.

"She's waiting at my house."

Justin stopped. "No. Shit. I don't want her to see me like this, not when I've been in a cage for three days like some animal."

"We can stop at your place and let you clean up." Deanna squeezed his arm again. "Gods, Justin, I was so scared. Why did you—?"

"Long story."

"I want to hear every word of it."

Justin smiled down at her. He was exhausted, hurting, and still worried, but his happiness at seeing Deanna was rendering all that irrelevant.

"Your mom?"

"Is fine." Deanna stopped on the street, a quiet turning that would take them to Justin's apartment. "She's really fine. She's still on Ariel with Reda, but she's going shopping and out to dinner . . ." Deanna trailed off, tears wetting her cheeks.

Justin wiped away one of the tears, kissing it from his fingertip. "I'm glad."

"Thank you. Thank you, Justin."

"Anytime, sweetheart." Justin gathered Deanna to him, despite them being in the street, and pressed a kiss to the top of her head. "I'd do anything for you, Deanna. Anything. And then I'd do it all over again."

* * * * *

Sybellie looked horrified when Justin walked into Deanna's apartment, Justin with his face bruised and lined with weariness. But, Deanna saw with satisfaction, Sybellie's horror was concern for Justin, not disgust that her father had been taken in like a criminal.

The three of them talked for a long time, Deanna telling them about her mother's treatment on Ariel, Sybellie and Justin filling her in on how Justin had finally approached Sybellie on the campus.

"I'm glad he did," Sybellie said, resting an affectionate hand on Justin's arm. "I feel silly now that I was afraid to meet him."

"It was a big step," Deanna said.

"It was." Sybellie drew a breath. "But I've taken it. Now I want to meet my mother."

Deanna nodded. "I'll arrange it."

Justin shot her a look of surprise, then nodded in understanding. Lillian had stated that she didn't want to see her daughter, but Deanna had the feeling that if Lillian met Sybellie, she'd fall in love with the girl and be glad she'd met her. It was worth a shot.

They talked more, Deanna's heart growing warmer as time wore on. The three of them were getting to know each other, sharing lives. When Deanna's mother got back, they'd share more. Kayla would like Justin—she already did.

Deanna's only fear now was that Justin, having found Lillian and met Sybellie, would want to leave Bor Narga. There was nothing to keep him here, and he had enough money to pay a transport captain to sneak him off planet without anyone being the wiser.

Sybellie could travel to see him anytime she wished—there were no off-planet restrictions on her.

When Sybellie decided she'd better go home, Justin stood with her and pulled her into his arms.

"You are so beautiful, Syb. Thank you."

"For what? Deanna got you out of jail."

"For wanting to see me."

Sybellie hugged him in return. "Why shouldn't I want to see you? You're my dad." And she was gone, off in her private transport back to her cushy home on the Vistara.

Justin watched her hovercar disappear into the streets, a strange, intense look on his face. He swung around to face Deanna, hands curling to fists. "Deanna . . ."

"Justin?"

He grabbed her by the shoulders and propelled her back inside, pushing her through the apartment block and into her empty flat.

As the door closed on them, Deanna swung around. "Justin? Are you all right?"

He growled and came at her. The silks she'd bought on Ariel tore from her body, and then Justin's mouth was on her skin. He kissed her throat, neck, breasts—frantically, as though fearing he'd never have the chance again. Then he raised his head, his eyes as blue as Ariel's shimmering lakes.

Justin swept her, naked, into his arms and nearly ran with her into her bedroom. It took him less than ten seconds to rip off his tunic and leggings, and then he came down to the bed with her, ready for her as soon as they both hit the mattress.

"I missed you," he said. No whispering, no teasing, just a clear statement in a plain voice. "I'll never let you leave without me again, Deanna. Never."

"I'll stay," she said breathlessly. "I'll stay. I missed you so much."

"Deanna . . ."

Justin closed his eyes, his body taking over. No level-two games, no laughing play—only Justin and Deanna, man and woman, meeting body to body.

Deanna opened herself to him, Justin's large cock finding all the spaces inside her and filling them up. But her orgasm was coming, too soon, *too soon.*

"I love you, Justin!" Her vision narrowed to nothing but Justin's face, his hot blue eyes, his sun-dark skin, his beautiful mouth. "I love you."

"Deanna." Justin skimmed his fingers over her face, his gaze fixed on her and her alone. "I love you. I love you, my beautiful, sweet, wicked little patroller. I looovvve . . ."

The word dragged out then was lost in the sounds of his coming.

"I love you," he whispered as he wound down, then he was kissing her, the warm kisses of after-loving. "I love you."

Deanna touched his face, her heart full, and pulled him down for a long and wonderful kiss.

Chapter Twenty-Two

"So," Rees said to Justin in Judith's bar the next day. "Ready to start again?"

"I'm not in a big hurry." Justin looked across the room to where Deanna and Katarina were discussing in detail with Brianne, Talan, and Elisa everything they'd done on Ariel. "But yeah. As long as I can take Deanna with me, as long as Sybellie can visit, I'm good with wherever you want to go."

"Good." Rees sipped ale with an air of relief. "I'm glad for you, actually. You were messed up. Now all we need is Mitch."

"Who is where?"

Rees shrugged. "Who the hell knows? He comes and goes. Judith doesn't know where he went, which is pissing her off."

They both glanced at Judith, who was wiping the top of her bar and scowling at it. When Braden thunked his elbows on the counter and gave her a wink, she swatted him with the cloth and snapped at him to get his damn arms off her clean bar.

"Hope she doesn't implode," Justin said.

"Used to be, she'd relieve her loneliness and horniness with Shareem," Rees said. "Now she's promised to be exclusive to Mitch, and he doesn't keep her in the loop. That's going to be interesting."

"One way of putting it." Justin's body relaxed of its own accord, which told him that Deanna was coming to him. He could always sense her now.

"Walk me home?" Deanna asked. "I want to fix up the place before my mom gets back. I bought some new pictures and a couple pieces of furniture on Ariel. That is, Katarina bought them for me and wouldn't take no for an answer. She's very generous."

"All the Shareem's ladies are generous," Rees said, opening his arm to scoop in Talan, who'd walked over with Deanna.

"We have to be," Talan said. "To put up with you."

Rees rumbled something and then ceased to be interested in Justin.

Justin got out of his seat and took Deanna's hand, steering her away from the table. "I have something to show you before we go to your apartment. To celebrate us becoming lifemates."

Deanna blinked. "Lifemates? When did you ask me to be your lifemate?"

Justin looked around at his friends, who'd heard, and who were now watching with interest. "I'm asking you now. Will you be?"

Deanna's lips were parted, pink moisture behind them. Justin could lean down and take that open mouth, but he wanted her answer.

She smiled suddenly, and the cold inside him fled. "Yes."

"Hot damn!" Braden said from the bar, and the others cheered or applauded. "Better get more beer, Judith."

"Sure thing." Judith grinned, her sour look gone. "I'll put it on your tab, Braden. Congratulations, Justin. *Your* beer, and Deanna's, are on me."

"Can't stop. Have something we need to do." Justin laced his arm around Deanna, pulling her to his side. "See you all."

"What?" Deanna asked as Justin half-dragged her out the door with him. "Why can't we stop?"

"I have to show you my surprise."

Justin wanted to run down the street, maybe with a few back flips to show his happiness, but he made himself walk calmly. They didn't need the attention of the patrollers right now.

But he wanted to shout to the world that he was in love, that the woman by his side had agreed to be his lifemate. The roasting Bor Nargan sun had never seemed so gentle, the dusty streets never so dazzling with color.

Deanna was a little dizzy with happiness herself. The sun glaring down didn't help, so she felt lightheaded by the time they stopped on a back street in front of a dingy warehouse door.

"What are we doing here?" she asked.

Justin took out a keycard, opened the door, and guided Deanna inside. The door shut behind them, and he led her down a dim, sand-gritty hall to a door at the far end, which opened at his command.

"Oh," Deanna said as she walked through.

Another world opened before her. She found herself inside a lush green maze filled with heady-smelling flowers, fountains, and hidden waterfalls, the plants stirred by breezes under the mist-disguised ceiling.

"What is this place?" she asked in wonder.

"Calder's dungeon."

Dungeon? Justin led her through too quickly for Deanna to pause for the beauty she found around every corner, but this didn't look like a dungeon to her. Calder had created a garden paradise.

At the end of the maze, another door led into a huge, darkened room, in the middle of which reposed a bed on a platform. The bed was dressed in scarlet satin, and a single red rose waited in its exact center.

"Justin, this is lovely. You'd never know all this was in here."

"Calder is the master of the secretive. I convinced him to let us use it to enjoy ourselves a while. I thought it would be more comfortable than my pint-sized bedroom."

"Or mine." Deanna opened her arms and spun around. The walls were dark, the air freshly scented, the ceiling shimmering with pinprick lights like stars. "It's gorgeous."

Justin watched her quietly, making no move to start undressing her or bring out toys. He simply let her dance around, enjoying herself.

"Remember when I talked to you about watching?" he asked. "How stimulating I said it could be?"

Deanna came to rest against the bed. "Yes?" She still wasn't sure she would like that.

"I thought, to give you a taste of what it's like, you could watch . . . us."

He clicked a handheld she hadn't noticed him picking up, and the walls blossomed screens. They were blank, black windows to nothing.

"Calder has cameras in amazing places. He can focus them anywhere." Justin came to her. "He and I spent a week figuring out the right angles. You can watch anything we do, while we do it. Such as . . ."

He cupped her face with one hand and at the same time, clicked the handheld. One of the large screens came up with an image of the two of them, her face and his, close together.

Justin licked her lips, and she saw it all behind him, his tongue tracing her mouth, then his eyes half-closing as he moved his hand to the nape of her neck and kissed her.

Another screen came on to show the back of her, and Justin undoing her coverall. The coverall crumpled to the floor, Justin's large hand moving down to cover her silk-clad buttocks.

The next screen glowed to life as he continued undressing her. Deanna watched him kiss his way down her torso as he slid her sheath and leggings from her. He leaned in to lick her bared clit, and a screen blossomed to show Deanna's pussy, his mouth closing on it, her fingers curling, Justin's tongue flickering on her clit.

When Justin undressed, she got to see close-ups of his body, especially his tight, fine ass. When he laid her on the bed, the remaining screens came on, showing that he'd rigged one to display where they joined. She watched in fascination as his dark and rigid cock slid into her, penetrating her.

She got to watch his ass move as he worked into her, saw his mouth find her breast, his eyes closing in concentration. Another screen showed Deanna's fingers thread his dark hair, her legs coming up to wrap around him.

Then she forgot about the cameras, and lay back to enjoy the feeling of Justin's weight on her body, his heat on her skin, the power of him inside her. This love was hot, raw, sensual.

She whimpered when Justin withdrew, but her excitement sped again when he turned her over, pulling her back on her hands and knees.

Screens at Deanna's eye level lit with images of Justin's large cock, shining with lube and her come, poised to drive back inside her. She saw her own face, relaxed in pleasure, half-smiling at the anticipation of what was to come.

They showed Justin, his big hands on her hips, face intent with need, and his cock, slick, hard, and impossibly large, sliding smoothly into her.

When she felt him move all the way in, she closed her eyes, not caring about anything but the feeling of Justin ramrod hard inside her, the gentle slap of his balls on her ass, the contrast of his hot, hard body with the cool satin beneath her hands and knees.

The feelings took her over the top just as Justin groaned with them. She felt the rapid pulses of his coming, his seed scalding into her.

Perhaps that seed would give them both another joy. Deanna hoped it with all her heart.

They fell together onto the bed, Justin still inside her, Deanna laughing. The screens showed her smiling, Justin naked, his bronzed body beautiful as it covered hers.

The room started to dim, and Deanna realized that the screens were flicking off, one by one, as their excitement spun down. Finally, only one remained, showing Deanna and Justin twined together, he spooned behind her, her small body fitting into the curve of his much larger one.

"Wow," Deanna said.

His breath was warm in her ear. "You liked that?"

"Maybe we should redo your place with cameras."

Justin chuckled. "Maybe we should."

More silence as they wound into the comfort of the bed. Deanna was perfectly warm, the room's temperature exactly regulated for a spent woman with a Shareem curled around her.

"You're going to leave Bor Narga, aren't you?" Deanna asked after a time.

She felt his little start, but he only said, "Hmm?"

"You can't want to stay here, and now, you don't need to. You've done what you came here to do."

"That's true." Justin drew his thumbnail beneath one of her nipples. "But when I go, you're coming with me. We're lifemates now."

Deanna's heart beat faster, happiness threatening to drown her. "Just try and stop me."

"Mmm, that might be fun. I could tie you down and leave you here, then come back to lick you all over, then come back again to fuck you . . ."

Deanna laughed. "You are such a level two."

His eyes narrowed. "How would you know?"

"Katarina and I talked a lot on our trip. She gave me details about all the levels—she's learned much, being medic to the Shareem. And Brianne has some interesting tales about what it's like with a level one versus a level three."

"The ladies have naughty mouths."

"About Shareem, yes." Deanna touched her abdomen and lost her smile. "You had Sybellie. Do you think it's possible for me too?"

"To have my child?" Justin slid his hand over hers where it rested on her belly. "I hope so. We'll see, won't we? I told Katarina to stop giving me the sterility inoculations."

"Good." Her heart warmed. Justin had given her enough of his seed today that something might come of it.

"We can always make sure," Justin said.

She felt her smile return. "I'm exhausted. Can we rest a *few* more minutes?"

"Sure. What we did was recorded, if you want to watch it again."

She jumped. "Recorded?" Her face heated. "I'm not sure I want to see that. I probably looked ridiculous."

Justin's eyes went soft. "You were beautiful."

"Though it wouldn't be bad to see you again. Especially that cock."

"Not what I'll be looking at." Justin reached for the handheld on the bedside table and clicked a few buttons. "Here we go. Lie back and enjoy."

The screens lit with images. She got to again watch Justin undress himself, the cameras showing every detail of his body, from strong fingers to wide chest, to tight backside, to long, thick cock.

He was right about watching — seeing Justin take her, Deanna looking up at him, her eyes heavy, made her warm and excited.

"See?" Justin tossed aside the handheld. "It can be a lot of fun. Now, let's show those people on the screen how much better we can do it."

He rolled Deanna into the mattress, hands pinning her wrists. Deanna rose to meet him, laughing as he laughed.

"I love you, Justin."

He nuzzled her. "I love you too, sweet Deanna," he said. "Thank you for setting me free."

Her smile widened. "But I arrested you."

"And as soon as you clicked those cuffs around me, you in that sexy coverall, I knew you were the woman for me."

"Oh, bullshit."

"Absolutely true. If you don't believe me, you can put me in the cuffs again."

Deanna laughed. "I love you."

"I love you, sweetheart." He closed his eyes as he slid inside her. "Deanna, my world."

Deanna held him close, and then loving took over, and then, bliss.

End

About the Author

Award-winning author Allyson James is a pen name of *New York Times* bestselling author Jennifer Ashley. Allyson has written more than 35 published novels and novellas in romance, urban fantasy, and mystery under the names Jennifer Ashley, Allyson James, and Ashley Gardner. Her books have been nominated for and won Romance Writers of America's RITA (given for the best romance novels and novellas of the year), several *RT BookReviews* Reviewers Choice awards (including Best Urban Fantasy and Best Shapeshifter Romance), Prism awards for her paranormal romances, and Passionate Plume and CAPA awards for her erotic romances.

More about Allyson's books can be found at the website: www.allysonjames.com

Or email Allyson at allysonjames@cox.net

Books in the Shareem series
Rees
Maia & Rylan (short story)
Rio
Aiden & Ky
Calder
Braden
Justin

Books in the Stormwalker series
Stormwalker
Firewalker
Shadow Walker
Nightwalker (forthcoming)
And more to come!

CPSIA information can be obtained
at www.ICGtesting.com
Printed in the USA
FSOW01n1604221217
42686FS